A Voice
from the Border

A Voice
from the Border

Pamela Smith Hill

Holiday House / New York

Library of Congress Cataloging-in-Publication Data
Hill, Pamela Smith.
A voice from the border / by Pamela Smith Hill. — 1st ed.
p.   cm.
Summary: Living in the border state of Missouri during the Civil
War, fifteen-year-old Reeves tries to understand her father's
decision regarding their slaves.
ISBN 0-8234-1356-X (hardcover: alk. paper)
1. Missouri—History—Civil War, 1861–1865—Juvenile fiction.
[1. Missouri—History—Civil War, 1861–1865—Fiction. 2. Fathers
and daughters—Fiction. 3. Slavery—Fiction. 4. Afro-Americans—
Fiction. 5. United States—History—Civil War, 1861–1865—
Fiction.]   I. Title.
PZ7.H557215Vo   1998   97-37251   CIP   AC
[Fic]—dc21

For Mom, Dad,
and
Angela

Acknowledgments

I OFFER MY SINCERE thanks to the many people who have helped me research, organize, and write this book. Nearly everyone I know has provided encouragement, support, and assistance as I toiled over this project for far too long.

I am especially indebted to Oregon Literary Arts, who helped fund my research in southwest Missouri and northwest Arkansas. The entire staff at the Shepard Room in the Springfield-Greene County Library provided invaluable research assistance. So did Southwest Missouri State University professors Dr. Katherine Lederer and Dr. William Piston. And how can I begin to thank Aaron Wahlquist, who loaned me a PowerBook when I needed it most?

I'm eternally grateful to the members of both my critique groups, who listened to countless versions of every chapter and helped me craft a better book. In particular, I'm indebted to Carmen T. Bernier-Grand, Carolyn Conahan, and Graham Salisbury, who read early versions of the manuscript; and to Dorothy Morrison, whose suggestion that I research the writings of Jessie Benton Frémont led to new insights into the Zagonyi Charge.

The staff at my neighborhood West Slope Community Library responded promptly and successfully to all my interlibrary loan requests, no matter how obscure.

My editor, Regina Griffin, and agent, Emilie Jacobson, gave me the time and opportunity to explore the characters in this book more deeply and more authentically. I am grateful for their professional counsel and wisdom.

This project would never have seen completion without the encouragement of my family. My grandfather's gift of a subscription to *Springfield! Magazine* rekindled my childhood aspirations to write about the Civil War in Missouri. My father loaned me his personal copies of several Missouri and Arkansas histories; he even braved a snowstorm to drive me back and forth to the Springfield library during my final week of location research. My husband and daughter endured my private battles with the Civil War and provided a peaceful environment in which to work.

And finally, one last thank-you to Heather, my flat-coated retriever and old friend, who spent hours at my side and eased the loneliness of writing while I wrote this book.

A Voice
from the Border

CHAPTER 1

Yesterday I slipped over to see Mrs. Phelps, and that vile Federal officer who rides a black charger tipped his hat to me again. It is very <u>provoking</u>. I'm not interested in such foolishness.

—The Diary of Margaret Reeves O'Neill,
July 14, 1861

"IT ISN'T LUCKY to talk about your own death." Mama's voice swept up the stairs like a stormy March wind. I set down my pen and looked over at Lucy, who was admiring herself in her new sprigged muslin for this afternoon's social.

"Daddy must be talking about his will again," I said.

Lucy met my gaze in the mirror, her eyes scared and big. "I think it's noble what Daddy's doing. I just wish he wouldn't talk about it so much."

I almost said everybody was talking about dying these days. But that wasn't so. Everybody was talking about *fighting,* not *dying.* Though as Daddy said, it amounted to the same thing.

"Folks are just caught up in all the glory of war right now," he'd said the night before at dinner with the Campbells. "But after the first battle comes, we'll see how the people of Missouri really feel about this war—after glory steals life from both sides."

"I won't hear any more of this talk, Gaylen." Now Mama's voice was sharp, insistent. "I don't care what your last will and testament says. Besides, our servants will stay on—no matter what happens in this war."

"You mean our slaves, my dear. They are not our servants."

"Whatever you call them," Mama replied firmly, "they're staying right here with us, where they belong."

The door to Daddy's library closed, and Mama's skirts swooshed around the landing, up the stairs. She burst into our bedroom, her face flushed, ringlets of golden hair damp against her forehead.

"Put that diary away this instant, Margaret Reeves," she ordered. "You'll get ink all over your new gown." Then her voice softened, and she smiled. "Dear, you'll never get a beau if all the young men in Greene County think you're bookish."

I nodded obediently and put my diary away, but as she turned toward Lucy, I slipped a small notebook and pencil into the secret pocket I'd had Juneau sew into the side seam of my new watered silk.

Mama looked at Lucy's reflection and smiled. "My, that new muslin is nice, Lucinda. Before you know it, you'll be wearing real hoop skirts like Reeves."

Lucy's face was still pale, her eyes wide. "Why does Daddy talk so much about his will?"

Mama's voice went flinty cold. "Don't speak of such things, Lucinda. It isn't proper."

"He's going to volunteer with the governor's militia, isn't he?"

Though both Mama and Daddy had tried to shield Lucy from politics, she knew as well as anybody that Governor Jackson expected all loyal Missourians to arm themselves against President Lincoln's invading Federal army. The truth was there for the knowing like smoke in the wind.

"Lucy, your daddy is going to stay right here with us in Springfield. He has no plans to leave us all alone." Mama took a deep breath to regain what she called a lady's proper composure. Then she tried to smile. "Now, girls, it isn't your place to worry about politics. Calm yourselves and think pleasant, summertime thoughts." She whisked toward the doorway. "I'll send Juneau up for you in a few minutes. Reeves, be sure you wash the ink from your hands and rinse them in rosewater. Soft hands soften the heart of one's true love."

Lucy waited until Mama's footsteps reached the hall downstairs, then she quivered. "Do you think Daddy is really going to stay home with us?"

I turned away. Lucy was awfully young, just eleven years old. But Daddy had confided in me when I was younger, and sometimes I wondered if I knew more about him at fifteen than Mama did at thirty-two.

From the road out front came the hard, tromping sounds of men marching. Federal volunteers—hundreds of German immigrants from St. Louis, perfectly in step. I ran to the window and leaned out for a closer look. I never tired of watching them. They had run Governor Jackson out of the Capitol. Now they planned to run him out of Missouri, to free the whole state of Secessionists who supported President Davis's new Confederacy.

A Federal soldier on horseback broke rank below and reined in his dusty, black horse under my window. The same officer I'd been seeing all that week! He tipped his hat and waved. I felt my face flush and backed away. Now he knew where I lived. What liberties would he take next? If all Federal officers were so ill-bred, maybe there was some merit to this war after all.

Then it dawned on me.

If Daddy joined this war, I'd have more to fear from that young man than flirtatious winks and waves. I thought of the carbine strapped across his saddle, his saber gleaming in the sun.

"Tell me the truth, Reeves," Lucy pleaded, her eyes filling with tears. "I know Daddy has told you what he aims to do. Is he going to join Governor Jackson? Is that why he talks about his will so much? *Please*. I have to know."

I summoned up one of Mama's favorite phrases. "A gentleman should always speak his own mind. I'm sorry, Lucy, but Daddy will have to speak for himself."

"It isn't fair!" Lucy pouted and pulled out one of her yellow hair ribbons. "Daddy always confides in you. Why doesn't he talk to me?" She threw the ribbon at my feet. "It isn't fair."

I reached into my secret pocket and felt for my notebook. It was comforting, filled with things I *knew*, things I'd seen and understood. Like the color of a crescent moon in July. Or Juneau's recipe for applesauce pie. But my world was changing and so was Daddy.

Daddy didn't like slavery. He'd once called it, "a monstrous institution." When the news first arrived about the firing on Fort Sumter, he'd told me, "It's already in the will, Margaret Reeves. No matter what happens in this coming conflict, our people will be free after I've passed on."

Yet if Daddy had to choose sides today, he'd join forces with Governor Jackson's Secessionists and fight Mr. Lincoln's troops outside our door. Daddy's loyalty was to his home state, and Virginia had chosen to secede. Already Daddy's brothers—Uncle James and Uncle Bertram—had regiments of their own back in Virginia.

"A man must stand up for his home and family," Daddy told me once. "Nothing in all the world is more important."

"But isn't this war about slavery?" I'd asked, watching dozens of troops parade past our front porch. "Isn't that why so many states have already seceded from the Union?"

"Nearly all of our friends are slaveholders, Reeves," Daddy had tried to explain. "But think how many have aligned themselves with President Lincoln's Union. The question of slavery has little to do with their loyalties. At least, for now." But his voice had sounded hollow and small.

Our bedroom door swung open and there stood Daddy himself. The most handsome man in the world, as Mama liked to say.

"You look mighty pretty, girls, but why so solemn?"

Lucy ran to him and he folded her in his arms.

"All those mean German soldiers," she sobbed. "And—and you. Writing a will! Oh, Daddy, don't go!"

"Now, Lucinda. There's nothing to worry about. A man with a family has to be prepared." He pulled her close and stroked her hair. "The war makes no difference. I just want you girls—and your mama—to be secure if something happens to me."

Lucy wailed. "But that's just it! Are you going to enlist? Please, Daddy. Tell me true!"

"I have no plans right now to fight—for either side." He paused and looked at me, then took a crinkled envelope from his pocket. "Claib offered me a commission last night."

I snatched the envelope from his hand and scanned the letter.

July 13

Dear Gaylen,

Low on ammunition, foodstuffs, and battle-ready volunteers. But prepared to offer you a commission as Captain in our cavalry under the command of General Sterling Price, another gentleman from Virginia. I leave immediately on a Mission of State in Richmond with President Davis, but General Price is prepared for your acceptance of this commission.

The Honorable Claiborne Jackson
Governor of Missouri
Cowskin Prairie, McDonald County, Missouri

Affixed at the bottom of the torn and crumpled page was the official seal of the State of Missouri.

I looked up at Daddy, full of questions I couldn't ask in

front of Lucy. So I pulled him aside and whispered, "How—
when did you get this?"

His eyes twinkled. "Mrs. Campbell smuggled it across
Union lines swept up in the back of her hair. She passed it
under the dinner table last night. You'd be surprised what
some ladies can accomplish, Reeves, whether their loyalties
be Union or Confederate."

Old Mrs. Campbell! A Confederate spy!

"You never tell *me* your secrets, Daddy," Lucy said, pout-
ing. "Never."

Daddy looked straight at her, his eyes suddenly sad and
grim. "These are dangerous times, and there are some things
in this new world that little girls like you don't need to
know about yet."

Then he touched my arm and whispered, "Mrs. Campbell
is a brave woman, Margaret Reeves. Remember that."

But all I could think about was Daddy's commission.
"What will you do?" I asked.

Daddy's fine, brown eyes met mine. "Time will tell," he
said.

CHAPTER 2

Off to the little church in the glade they went, hampers brimming with the fruits of summer. What peace! What joy! What harmony!

—from "The Happy Picnickers,"
Margaret Reeves O'Neill,
July 14, 1861

WE WERE ALREADY a quarter of an hour late to the social, but Mama still fussed over my new watered silk.

"It isn't quite right around the neck is it, Juneau?" Mama pulled at a piece of Spanish lace. "I wish your neck weren't so scrawny, Reeves. Then we wouldn't have to cover it up like this."

She motioned to Juneau, who stood in the corner of the bedroom, her lovely face as smooth as polished mahogany. I could never tell how Juneau felt about us, though she'd been with Mama since they were both little girls. "My right hand," Mama liked to say. But even though Juneau worked hard for us and never complained, I sometimes thought she'd just as soon see us dead as alive. Except for Daddy.

"Stand still, Miz Reeves." Juneau's voice was deep and even as she snipped at my lace fluff with her razor-sharp sewing scissors.

I swallowed hard and looked across the room. Daddy sat at my writing desk, reading the last pages of the picnic story I'd finished the night before for my portfolio. I wasn't sure which worried me more: Juneau's sharp scissors snipping away around my neck or Daddy's opinion of my newest story. He turned the last page, and it rustled like dry leaves in September.

I held my breath.

Daddy got up and walked to the window, his hands clasped behind his back. Lucy moved into his place and began reading. I hated it when she read what I wrote.

Finally Daddy turned. "You've been reading too many stories by Mrs. Stowe," he said gently. Then his eyes met mine. "Find your own voice, Reeves; do not imitate the path others have taken."

Lucy looked up and giggled. She liked it when Daddy criticized me.

"But Mrs. Stowe is an accomplished writer, Daddy. Her stories have kindled emotions as no other authoress ever has."

"But they're not *your* stories, Reeves. Think of your writer's notebook and your diary. Now there's where the real Margaret Reeves O'Neill comes shining through."

"You've read Reeves's diary?" Mama whirled, her skirts filling the room with the fragrance of lavender. "Why, Gaylen, she's never let me read it and I'm her own mama." She whirled back and glared at me. "What kind of a girl refuses to share her innermost thoughts with her mama, then pours out her soul to her daddy? I've never of heard anything so . . . so . . . unwholesome, or so improper, in all my born days."

Lucy stifled another giggle. Daddy crossed the floor and gently took Mama's arm.

"There's nothing improper about it at all, Vashti. I merely looked at a few writing exercises Reeves copied out in her diary. You'd find them tedious, dear. Not at all to your liking."

Mama looked at Daddy, then at me. "Well, if you say so. But I'd still like to see that diary of yours, Margaret Reeves. As I've said many times before, a mama can only plan a daughter's future if she knows her daughter's heart. I told my mama everything. Isn't that so, Juneau?"

"I remember you kept a few secrets of your own, Miz Vashti," Juneau replied, her voice smooth as sorghum molasses. "Like the Summertime Ball at Mayfair when you danced with Mista Howard Chestnut."

"Oh, tell us about it, Juneau. Do! Do!" Lucy twirled across the room, petticoats flying.

Mama glared at Juneau, the way she always did when Juneau bested her in front of us all. "I'll take care of Miss Lucy's sash myself, Juneau." Mama's voice was soft as a feather pillow, hard as clay. "Then we'd best be off, Gaylen. I do believe we're already a half hour behind our time."

JUNEAU'S SON Hector was waiting outside with the open carriage. He was my age, tall and strong and well spoken—though he kept quiet when Mama was around. "His mind has been poisoned with a fatal potion," she always said, because ages and ages ago, Hector's daddy, who'd been owned by Lester Grimes across town, had run off with a band of Jayhawkers—antislavery men from Kansas who robbed and murdered slaveholders in their beds.

"If it weren't for Juneau," Mama liked to say, "I have no doubt but what Hector would join up with those Jayhawkers, too, and burn our very home to the ground—with a smile on his face."

But I agreed with Daddy. Hector was smart and dependable.

He helped Mama into the carriage. Then me. Then Lucy. Juneau climbed in herself. Though we all knew how dear Hector was to her, she never displayed tenderness when the two of them were working together. Hector handed her a big hamper filled with two blackberry pies and a burnt-sugar cake.

"I'll need that, too," she said, pointing to a carpetbag stuffed with Mama's "beauty supplies": brushes, combs, fans, smelling salts, and extra lace fluffs in case any of us spilled lemonade down the front of our dresses that afternoon. Wordlessly, Hector hoisted the bag, jumped onto the carriage, and took up the reins.

Daddy mounted Trooper, his blood bay stallion, and motioned for Hector to follow. Daddy's man Hiram stood out on our wide front porch waving good-bye as if we were leaving on a long journey. But Hiram was always like that, as tender and warm as a soft summer night.

*   *   *

I ACHED to be riding beside Daddy on one of our prized plantation pacing horses, as I usually did. When Daddy had a fine lady's mare ready for sale, I'd ride it to important social functions and impress potential buyers with its suitability for ladies. But Mama said I was getting far too old to go to socials, fairs, and balls wearing a riding habit and riding sidesaddle.

Our carriage hit the big rut on the corner of Jefferson and St. Louis Streets. "Don't try to keep up with Mr. O'Neill, Hector," Mama commanded. "And drive with more caution." She adjusted her hoops. "All this dust could ruin the effect of Miss Reeves's watered silk. I *knew* we should have brought dusters."

"You'd have smothered in dusters, Miz Vashti, and you know it." Juneau reached into the carpetbag and handed me a fan. It smelled of her favorite verbena sachet.

"Don't contradict me, Juneau." Mama raised her parasol. "As you well know, a lady always arrives at her destination as fresh as a daisy, no matter how ruthless the elements."

It *was* hot. And dry. Dust swirled up from the street like smoke in a smokehouse and settled on our clothes, our skin, our hair. It was worse when we got to the Square. Mr. Jenkins's pigs had gotten loose again, and they churned up more dust than a team of foul-tempered mules. A small group of German soldiers waved as we drove by. Otherwise, the square was curiously deserted—at midday on a Saturday. Where were all the merchants—and their customers? Where were the regiments of Federal soldiers who usually gathered there on Saturday afternoons? And where was Mr. Jenkins? When his pigs got out, he usually wasn't far behind.

"Why is it so quiet today?" Lucy whined. She liked to be seen, especially when she was looking her best. "Surely, not everybody's going to the social. The Reverend Casey didn't invite the Methodists or the Baptists, did he, Mama?"

Daddy cantered back on Trooper and pulled up beside the carriage. I could tell by the way he squinted off into the distance that he was worried.

"I wonder if the Reverend Mr. Casey invited a few of his Yankee friends to our little gathering?" Daddy said softly. Then he spurred Trooper down Boonville Hill, out toward church.

Mama slowly lowered her parasol and handed it to Juneau. "Speed up, Hector," she ordered. "Keep Mr. O'Neill in sight and don't mind the dust."

"Yes, ma'am." Hector clicked to the horses and we lurched ahead. Mr. Jenkins's pigs squealed and scurried out of our way.

We sped down Boonville Hill in a cloud of red dust, past the whitewashed houses that got smaller and smaller as we moved farther from the square. Mama's face was pale and she fanned herself furiously. Lucy held on to her bonnet; Juneau steadied the bouncing hamper. Then up ahead, Daddy and Trooper disappeared around the sharp corner at the bottom of Boonville Hill.

"Faster, Hector," Mama ordered, waving her fan.

We bumped down the last quarter mile, then rounded the corner. Daddy was just ahead of us, behind a stand of walnut trees that screened the road from the church. He motioned for us to stop.

A bank of uniformed soldiers had circled the church. I recognized Mr. Jenkins, Mr. Crawford, and Mr. Graves with the Reverend Casey—all Union men. They stood out front, dividing the picnickers into three groups. One large group of men, women, and children gathered under a sycamore. A smaller group of women and children huddled on the front steps. The third group—all men with their hands tied behind them—stood out back in a stand of dogwoods. Among them I recognized Mr. Butler and Mr. Cooper— Daddy's friends, men who sympathized with the Confederate cause, with Governor Jackson and General Price.

It was much too quiet for a picnic.

"So it's come to this," Daddy murmured. "A church divided against itself."

I felt my stomach in my throat. Daddy's friends tied up like criminals. . . . I looked at Daddy, but he wouldn't look at me.

He swung out of the saddle and walked back to the carriage. "They've forced my hand at last, Vashti," he said. "I have no choice but to act." He took off his hat and kissed her full on the mouth. Mama started to cry.

"Listen to me, Vashti." His voice was stern but warm. "You and the girls will have to go on. Do what these people tell you to do. Tell them I'm coming along later." Daddy turned and looked right at me. "Do you understand?"

I nodded.

"Make sure you all tell the same story. Can you do that, Lucy?"

By this time, Lucy was crying, too. He kissed her swiftly. "Be brave, my little princess."

Then Daddy hugged me close and whispered, "I know you'll be brave."

I fought back tears and nodded again. The lump in my throat was so big I couldn't talk around it. But I wouldn't cry. I *wouldn't.*

"And Margaret Reeves, fill that portfolio of yours with new stories, your *own* stories," he said, squeezing my hand. "Have them waiting for me when I come home."

He kissed Mama again, then swung back on Trooper. "Take care of them, Juneau," he said, lightly touching her shoulder.

Then he was off, galloping up Boonville Hill.

My eyes filled with tears, and this time I couldn't stop them.

CHAPTER 3

It is hard to know what to think. Who is friend or foe? Who is right or wrong? Perhaps I should learn to accept acts of kindness where I find them, no matter who is the giver.

—Margaret Reeves O'Neill to her father, July 14, 1861

I WATCHED DADDY until he and Trooper disappeared over the hill. Then Juneau reached into Mama's carpetbag and produced a vial of smelling salts. She held it out for Mama.

"I'm fine, Juneau," Mama fussed. But she snatched the vial away and swirled it under Lucy's nose.

"Don't cry, little sweet pea. Be brave for your daddy."

Lucy's lips quivered and she gulped for air.

Mama glanced over at me.

"I'm fine, Mama," I said, wiping my eyes dry.

"Juneau, did you think to bring the rosewater?" Mama turned and smiled down at Lucy. "Nothing cures puffy eyes any better. It truly soothes the troubled brow."

Juneau dabbed a few drops of rosewater on a handkerchief and passed it around. It did feel good, so cool and sweet. Sometimes Mama knew what she was doing. She straightened Lucy's bonnet and fluffed up my lace.

The horses stamped and snorted, their tails switching at horseflies.

"Keep those horses still, Hector. I don't want to raise any attention just yet." Mama took a deep breath and closed her eyes. "Let us all hold hands, girls, and offer up a silent prayer for your daddy. May he reach General Price before these Yankees know he's missing."

I closed my eyes and reached across the carriage to take Mama's hand. But Juneau's hand—not Mama's—grasped mine. I squinted at Juneau and saw her lips moving silently. Was she truly praying for Daddy's safe escape—or for his capture? Then I glanced up at Hector. He'd turned around and was staring up the road almost as if he wanted to call Daddy back.

"All right," Mama said, raising her head. "Let's go."

The horses trotted past the walnut grove and swung into the open meadow, where a cluster of blue uniforms blocked the road. Instinctively, I reached for the notebook hidden in my pocket. I needed to write all of this down.

"You wouldn't have a pistol hidden in that pocket, would you, Miss?" It was that vile young officer who had winked at me that morning. He grinned and spurred his horse alongside our carriage. "I've heard tell that Ozark ladies are fierce and daring."

I pulled my hand out of my pocket quick as a June bug, and one of Mama's favorite phrases popped into my mind. "What I have in my pocket, sir, is none of your concern, because a gentleman always honors a lady's secrets."

"Margaret Reeves O'Neill!" Mama flashed. "A lady never flirts with a stranger."

I wanted to shout, "I'm not flirting!" But I didn't want to repeat the word *flirt* in front of that flirtatious officer. How could Mama think I'd flirt with anyone—especially a Federal soldier, especially now? I put my hand back in my pocket and ran my fingers over the smooth, cool leather of my notebook. The officer kept his eyes on me.

"We're not really strangers," he said smooth as corn silk. "For I've admired this young lady from afar since we got to Springfield. Now I see where she gets her beauty." He tipped his hat at Mama, then at me.

My cheeks burned. If all Yankees were like this, no wonder the South had seceded.

Mama ignored his flattery and waved toward the soldiers. "Why have your men surrounded our church?"

"I'm sorry for the inconvenience, madam, but we've had reports of Secessionist spies, some of them ladies, operating out of Springfield. So if you'll just proceed over there"—he pointed toward Mr. Jenkins, Mr. Graves, and Mr. Crawford—"you can take your loyalty oaths and be on your way."

A loyalty oath? I glanced at Daddy's friends—Mr. Butler and Mr. Cooper—standing bound and guarded behind the church. Their wives and children stood on the front steps, clearly apart from everybody else. They must have refused to take the oath. A tall, dark-haired woman on the top step turned and nodded at me. It was Mrs. Campbell. I knew she'd never swear loyalty to the Federal government, and I knew Mama wouldn't either. Couldn't. It would be like stabbing Daddy in the back.

"Young man, I believe this was meant to be a church function, not a military engagement." Mama raised her parasol. "Surely in the eyes of the Almighty, we are all His children on this fine Saturday afternoon. Isn't loyalty to our Lord all anybody needs in these trying times?"

Mr. Jenkins broke through the circle of soldiers and charged toward Mama. He wore a blue coat tied with a crimson sash. "Where's that husband of yours?"

"He'll be along later, Mr. Jenkins," I said quickly. I was better at making up stories than Mama. I could always make them sound real, even on the spur of the moment. "Trooper threw a shoe just as we crossed the square—in a rut where your pigs are rooting around again." I paused, hoping to buy Daddy more time. "Really, Mr. Jenkins, you've got to do something about those pigs. They're a public disgrace."

Mr. Jenkins leaned closer. His teeth were brown from years of chewing tobacco and he smelled like he should have removed his coat hours ago. "I didn't ask about my pigs, missy," he growled. "I asked about your daddy."

Lucy buried her head against Mama's shoulder. "You've scared my little one, Mr. Jenkins. Get away from our carriage."

He spit a big wad of tobacco and grinned up at the officer. "Best send some of your men back to town. O'Neill's secesh fer sure."

"But I told you," I said, trying to ignore the way the Federal officer stared at me, "Daddy'll be here directly. Before Mr. Stone there tunes up his fiddle."

"There ain't gonna be no fiddle music today, missy," Mr. Jenkins said, scowling at me. He started to jump up on the carriage.

Juneau blocked him with her carpetbag. "Get back, Mista Clifford Jenkins," she said, hard as stone. "Mista Gaylen'll be here like Miz Reeves says."

I stared at Juneau. She was no taller than Mama, a tiny woman in her fine black-cotton sateen and dark green turban. But she stood her ground, silent and threatening.

Finally the Federal officer spurred his horse forward and nudged Mr. Jenkins out of the way. "She's right, Jenkins. Let these ladies pass."

WE JOINED the end of a long line of people waiting to take their loyalty oaths from a short, one-armed brigadier general with gray whiskers. The line moved slowly, very slowly. A low drone of voices from the head of the line drifted down like a chorus of katydids. I watched as the Marshalls, Fosters, and Phillipses joined the ranks of pro-Union families. The Blackman, Smith, and Carpenter families were separated— the men tied up and marched into the ranks of Daddy's friends; their wives, daughters, and servants crammed around the church steps.

Finally, little Crystal Grimes, who stood just ahead of us in the line, turned and whispered, "Mama says they're gonna confuscate our property." Her eyes widened. *"Confuscate.* Oh, Reeves, tell me what that means!"

Mama's face went pale. So did Lucy's. If the army confiscated our property, where would we go? How would we live?

Mrs. Grimes pulled Crystal away and stared at Mama. "Where's your man, Vashti?" she hissed. "Has he finally found the guts to take a stand?"

Mama didn't answer. The Grimeses weren't our kind of people. Daddy always said if they hadn't been so cruel, Hector's daddy would never have turned Jayhawker. And before Mr. Grimes had left to join General Price, he'd called Daddy a coward. "Waitin' to see which way the wind blows? Not enough spine in ya, Gay, to straighten a wooly worm," he'd said. But now Daddy and Lester Grimes would be fighting on the same side. Somehow that didn't seem right.

Another hour drifted by. Juneau summoned Hector, and he brought us a big jar of lemonade from our picnic hamper. Mama let us all drink right from the jar. It was hot and sour, but wet, wet, wet. I let Lucy drain the last of it dry.

Finally Mrs. Grimes stepped up to the one-armed brigadier general. That vile, reckless, no-good scoundrel—the young officer who winked too much—stood by his side, along with Mr. Stone, Mr. Crawford, and the Reverend Mr. Casey.

"Mrs. Lester Grimes and daughters," the Reverend Mr. Casey stated clearly. "Secesh."

"Is this true, Mrs. Grimes, or are you and yours prepared to take an oath of loyalty to the United States of America?" asked the general.

"May God strike ya dead, Freeman Crawford. And you, too, Jim Stone. Turnin' on your own neighbors. And as fer you, Timothy Casey . . ." Mrs. Grimes spit over her shoulder and ground her heel in the dirt. "This is what I think of you."

Mama had always thought Mrs. Grimes coarse, but for the first time I thought there was something almost noble in the way she stood up for herself. I'd always believed I was a good judge of character, but today I had my doubts—about almost everybody.

"You bet I'm secesh," Mrs. Grimes bragged. "And my whole family, too. I won't take no oath. And you cain't make me."

She led Crystal, Susanna Lea, and their mammy, Auntie Cole, toward the cluster of women standing by the church steps. Suddenly Mrs. Grimes called back, "And you'll niver git that sorrel mare, Jim Stone. I've seen to it that an honest Confederate already has her."

Mr. Stone flinched.

Then it was our turn. We stepped forward, and the Reverend Mr. Casey said slowly, "Mrs. Gaylen O'Neill, daughters, and slavewoman Juneau. Sympathies"—he paused— "unknown."

All at once, Mr. Jenkins pushed through the line. "Unknown, my eye! I just come from their place. Gaylen's done lit out with the Campbell boys. Secesh, fer sure." He leered over at Mama. "A pretty piece of property, boys. Jist what you fellas been lookin' for. The best horseflesh in Greene County."

Mr. Crawford stared at Mama, and he looked truly grieved. But then he should have. The Crawfords had been to Sunday dinner with us I don't know how many times. And Mrs. Crawford had even visited me during my first spring term at the Fayetteville Ladies' Institute.

"Is this true, Vashti?" Mr. Crawford said slowly. "Has Gaylen joined General Price?"

Mama's voice was deep and clear. "I do not believe in taking oaths. 'For every one that sweareth shall be cut off,' " she quoted. "And I do not want to be cut off from the Grace of our Lord Jesus Christ."

I'd never been so proud of Mama. Daddy would have been proud of her, too.

"You have no choice, Vashti," Mr. Crawford murmured. "Please take the oath."

"I can't, Mr. Freeman," Mama said softly.

Mr. Jenkins grinned. Mr. Casey cleared his throat. Then a voice rang out—clear and fine and firm.

"No lady—Yankee or Reb—should be asked to compromise religious principles for the expediencies of government."

It was my vile Federal officer!

If I'd been the fainting kind, I would have swooned away right there and then. A complete stranger taking our part when even our friends stood against us.

"He's just chasing a petticoat, General," growled Mr. Jenkins. "O'Neill's secesh, I tell ya."

The brigadier general squinted up at the young officer. "You're one of General Lyon's aides, aren't you?"

"Yes, sir."

"You cain't do better'n that." The general paused, and, with his good arm, tipped his hat back. "This looks like a right honest family. You can go, ladies. But we'll be watchin' you, whether that man of yours joins Sterling Price or no."

Juneau led us back to the carriage, and Hector helped us all in. I looked back at the line still snaking toward the one-armed general. Would General Lyon's aide escort us home? I wanted to meet his gaze, to thank him somehow. Such a rare act of kindness—in such truly perilous times.

But he was gone, and I didn't even know his name.

CHAPTER 4

Hiram, Juneau, and even Hector are a mystery to me,
although we live our lives together as if we were family.
How do they feel about this war, and which side do they
pray for at night?
    —Writer's Notebook, Margaret Reeves O'Neill,
        July 14, 1861

THE SKY WAS DARK turquoise by the time we got home.
Lightning bugs danced among our dogwood trees, and pink
flashes of heat lightning fired up the sky way off to the south,
down toward Cowskin Prairie—and Daddy. I dragged myself out of the carriage as Hector lifted Lucy out. She'd fallen
asleep on the ride home.

Hiram met us on the front porch, a lighted lamp held
high in his hand. "He got clean away, Miz Vashti. Packed
three shirts, two pairs of trousers, and his fine summer frock
coat. But that man Jenkins was here."

"I know," Mama said, as if the words pained her.

Juneau handed the picnic hamper to Hiram. "Miz Vashti
and the girls need supper."

"It's on the table this very minute," he said.

Lucy still slept soundly in Hector's arms, and Mama directed Juneau to put her straight to bed. "She needs sleep

more than nourishment," Mama whispered, lightly touching the damp ringlets curled against Lucy's forehead.

Then Mama and I followed Hiram into the dining room. The table was spread for a feast. Fried chicken, ham, mashed potatoes and gravy, green beans from the garden, and the summer's first sweet corn, swimming in butter. Hiram took Juneau's blackberry pies and burnt-sugar cake from the hamper. He held out Mama's chair and motioned for her to sit down.

"Eat hearty, Miz Vashti."

But she just stared at the table as if she'd already eaten one big meal and couldn't face another. I wasn't hungry either.

"Did Daddy take anything with him other than clothes?" I asked, remembering how much Daddy loved fresh sweet corn.

Hiram shook his head. "Just his duelin' pistols, Miz Reeves, and his rifle."

Mama sighed. "Tell Cook to clear this all away. I'm not hungry." She paused, and suddenly her eyes shone bright. "But pack up the chicken, ham, and pies right away. You can find Cowskin Prairie in the dark, can't you, Hiram?"

"Lord, Miz Vashti, I could find it blindfolded. My wife's people came from off down there, and if you'll remember—" He stopped, for we all remembered.

Hiram's wife, Betsy, and their little baby girl had died the previous winter of influenza. Daddy and Hiram had carried their remains south in one of our wagons, over hard, icy, rutted roads, so that Betsy and her baby could be buried in her family plot. As I recalled, Mama had opposed Daddy's journey.

"Why put your own self at peril?" she'd argued. "One

grave is just as good as another. Betsy will never know the difference."

"But Hiram will," Daddy had answered, and that was all there was to it. Until now.

"Then you'll go?" Mama asked.

Hiram nodded.

"There'll be Federal patrols," I warned.

"Don't scare me none."

"Good." Mama smiled. "As I've said so many times before, a gentleman always needs his man beside him, Hiram. Even during times of war."

WHILE MAMA, Juneau, Hiram, and Cook packed supplies for Daddy, I slipped upstairs to my room and lighted a candle on my writing desk. Lucy's breathing came steady and even—she was fast asleep—so I quietly took out my pen and paper and began to write a letter to Daddy. How still and empty the house seemed without him. But forming my loneliness into words took the edge off and made me feel almost, *almost,* as if Daddy were right there beside me, looking over my shoulder.

JUST ABOUT midnight, I crept downstairs and found Mama and Hiram out on the front porch.

"You keep your eyes on Mr. Gaylen now," she said, giving him three gold pieces. "Do what you can to keep him out of harm's way."

There were tears in her eyes, tears in mine, tears in Hiram's. I slipped him Daddy's letter and hugged him tight. "Tell Daddy I miss him already."

"That I will, Missy Reeves," Hiram promised.

Juneau emerged from the house, carrying four bottles of her prime blackberry brandy, which she handed to Hiram. "Mista Gaylen always likes a brandy after sundown." Then she took a book out from under her arm. "Hector said Mista Gaylen would appreciate this."

I myself took the book from her hand. It was a heavy book of poems by England's Romantic writers. "I should have thought of this," I said, passing the book to Hiram and feeling a tinge of guilt—for it seemed our people knew Daddy every bit as well as Mama and me. Maybe better.

Hiram packed these last things away in Mama's big willow hamper, then swung into the saddle. He tipped his hat to us all, then turned his mule toward Jefferson Street.

"It'll be a wonder if he doesn't run off to the Jayhawkers," Mama said. But I knew she didn't believe that any more than I did.

Still, later that night, I realized it was a wonder. For if this war was about the abolition of slavery, then why would Hiram follow Daddy south? What was in his heart? What was in Juneau's? Hector's?

I lighted the candle by my bed and reached for my notebook. Yet the more I wrote that night, the less I understood. The lives of those closest to my family, the people who lived beside us like family, seemed impenetrable mysteries.

CHAPTER 5

*Cannon fire from Totten's Battery on East St. Louis
Street at 5:35 P.M. Artillery practice. Windows rattled
as if set off by a rumbling thunderstorm in November.
At times like these, Mrs. Phelps always says, "I wish
they'd save their ammunition for battle." Then I remind
her that those cannons would be directed at my daddy
when war comes. Mrs. Phelps is a kind woman at heart,
and she always says, "Forgive me, Reeves. I forget
myself."*

I think the whole world has forgotten itself.

—Writer's Notebook, Margaret Reeves O'Neill,
July 31, 1861

"I BELIEVE THESE should come to you from now on," Juneau
said, placing a package in my hands.

It was small but heavy, carefully wrapped. From Austen &
Clemens, St. Louis, Fine Booksellers. Daddy's regular book
order.

If he'd been home, Juneau would have delivered the package to his study, and he'd have shut out the world till suppertime. Then just at the closing of the day, he would summon
Lucy and me.

"For you, Lucy," Daddy would say, passing her a beautifully bound book of poems, perhaps by Mr. Longfellow or Mr. Wordsworth. Then he'd smile at me and present a thick, heavy novel from Mr. Dickens, Mr. Melville, or my favorite, Mr. Trollope. "I'll discuss this with your mama," he'd say sometimes, and then I knew it would be a good book.

Now with Daddy gone, Juneau must have thought the responsibility of reviewing a new book fell to me, not Mama. I was honored.

"Thank you, Juneau," I said. "Are there any more?"

"No, Miz Reeves. Just the one package."

I walked down the hall to Daddy's study and closed the door behind me. The smell of his cigars still lingered in the air, though he'd been gone over two weeks now. I shut the big windows that opened out to a grove of redbuds; I shut in my memories.

We hadn't heard from Daddy. Not a word, and that wasn't like him. It was as if the war—or at least Cowskin Prairie—had swallowed him whole. But Mrs. Campbell hadn't heard from her boys either, and she had four of them with General Price. Still, I wrote Daddy every day and tucked the letters into his portable writing case at night. *Someday he'll see them,* I told myself. *Someday I'll find a way to get them across Federal lines.*

I ran my hands over the package from Austen & Clemens. The label had been addressed in such a fine hand: MR. GAYLEN O'NEILL, JEFFERSON STREET, SPRINGFIELD, SOUTHWEST MISSOURI. A lump gathered in the back of my throat, and for a moment the lingering smell of Daddy's cigars stung my eyes. Should I leave the package unopened until Daddy returned?

I ran to the windows and threw them open, gulping in fresh air. Daddy was gone. I couldn't change that. But I couldn't stop living either. I tore the package open.

Adam Bede, a Novel in Three Volumes, by George Eliot.

Each volume was bound in fine, smooth brown leather. I turned to chapter one and read for the rest of the afternoon.

I HEARD Lucy calling for me, then Mama. Juneau had told them both that I'd gone out for afternoon calls and wouldn't be home till after supper. Then later, she'd slipped in with a tray. Cold ham with sweet potatoes, corn on the cob, and blackberry cobbler.

"You're your daddy's daughter, Miz Reeves. Even down to this—needin' time alone to your own self," she said. Then she was gone.

I hadn't expected such kindness from Juneau. She'd always reserved that for Daddy, though in truth, I didn't know why. For Juneau belonged to Mama. They'd been together as girls in North Carolina; then Juneau had been Grandfather Cameron Reeves's wedding present to Mama all those years ago.

Still, it was Daddy, only Daddy, who commanded Juneau's respect and admiration.

"It's because you pamper that boy of hers," Mama used to complain.

"He's a smart and promising young man," Daddy always argued.

"You're playing with fire," Mama would flash back. "Encouraging independent thinking."

"Everyone deserves their independence," Daddy would say, which would launch another argument about the will and his plan to free all our people when he died.

I pushed the tray away and reached for *Adam Bede.* It was a book Mama would never approve of. Characters who didn't follow the dictates of their "appropriate stations" in life, a woman who threw her reputation away, a child born out of wedlock. "A lady should never know about such things, much less read about them," Mama would have said. But it was a wonderful book, real and vivid and true.

The house shook as a round of cannon fire went off on East St. Louis Street. Artillery practice. We'd all gotten used to it. This sound of war was one of those things a lady should never have to know about, yet here it was almost on our doorstep. I reached for my notebook and took down the time of day, how intensely the windowpanes rattled, and my fear that one day those cannons would be directed at Daddy.

Maybe that's what drives a person to write. Maybe you're forced to know things you don't really want to know and you have to write it all down to make sense of it. If there is any.

And then I wondered if that's what Daddy meant by independent thinking, and why Mama feared it so.

CHAPTER 6

*The cases of plundering, wanton destruction of property,
and disregard of personal rights . . . have been disgrace-
ful to our troops, a violation of . . . orders, and contrary
to the purposes of the General Government. . . . By order
of General Lyon . . .*

    —J. M. Schofield, Acting Adjutant-General
    U.S. Army, Springfield, Missouri,
    July 1861

"I HAVE NEWS," Mrs. Campbell announced, arranging her skirts as she settled herself onto one of our narrow back-porch chairs. She reached into her wide willow basket and pulled out her knitting needles. I put Volume 3 of *Adam Bede* aside.

"If it's about Rebel troop movements, then I'd better excuse myself, Louisa," said Mrs. Phelps. "You know how we disagree on this issue." But Mrs. Phelps didn't stop knitting. Neither did Mama.

"I'm no fool, Mary Phelps." Mrs. Campbell peered over the top of her needles and smiled. "If I had news of the Confederacy and its noble fighting men, I'd speak with Vashti in private."

I slumped back in my chair, disappointed that the news wouldn't be about Daddy. How I ached for his low, rumbly laughter, the smell of brandy and cigars after supper.

Mrs. Campbell's granddaughter Little Lou and Lucy walked hand in hand down by the pond. They were too old to catch lightning bugs but too young to sit on the back porch knitting socks for soldiers—Mama and Mrs. Campbell for General Price's Southerners, Mrs. Phelps for General Lyon's Yankees. I didn't want to knit for soldiers on either side, so Mama let me knit socks for Hiram. I reached into my basket and pulled out a skein of purple wool, his favorite color.

"Well, are you going to give us the news or not?" Mama asked.

Mrs. Phelps's eyes twinkled. "What could you possibly have heard, Louisa Campbell, that my own husband hasn't already told me?"

Mrs. Phelps wasn't bragging, of course. It was just that her husband was the congressman from our district and a high-ranking officer who had the ear of Commanding General Nathaniel Lyon himself.

Mrs. Campbell stopped knitting and looked right at me.

"I know the name of Reeves's young officer."

Hiram's half-finished sock fell from my hands. I'd tried for days to find that officer and thank him for taking our part at the church social. I'd sent Hector out looking for him, since Mama no longer allowed Lucy and me to walk to the square. I'd even watched from my bedroom window, hoping he'd ride by on his big black horse and smile that provoking smile of his, but to no avail.

Mrs. Phelps laughed. "Louisa Campbell, I've known that boy's family all my life."

"Why didn't you tell me?" I asked, jumping to my feet.

"I didn't think your mama wanted you to know." Mrs. Phelps patted my hand and glanced at Mama. "But he's from one of the best and most literary families in all of St. Louis."

"Literary?" I gasped.

"*The Wilder Review*," she explained. "His father publishes it."

"Why, Daddy has a bookshelf full of *The Wilder Review*!"

"Sit down, Reeves," Mama said sharply, "and catch that ball of yarn before it rolls into the lily bed. I declare, when will you learn that a lady doesn't wear her feelings on her sleeve?"

"But we owe him, Mama. We owe him our gratitude and respect."

Mama didn't look at me, and for a minute or two no one spoke.

Finally I asked, "What is his name?"

"Percival Wilder," Mrs. Campbell said. "And he led a raid on the Grimes place this afternoon. His men took just about everything. Food, clothing, livestock. Down to the very last chicken. Nobody deserves such treatment, not even the Grimeses."

It felt as if some mighty and terrible weight had just fallen on my chest and crushed all the breath right out of my body. How could the same person divert disaster from one family, then bring it down on another?

"I tell you, Vashti," Mrs. Campbell was saying, "you have to be smarter than they are."

"Louisa's right." Mrs. Phelps set her knitting aside. "If you can't take their oath, then you have to take in their soldiers. Mr. O'Neill wouldn't want you and your girls to lose all this." She gestured out toward our wide backyard, which swept down the hill toward Daddy's horse barn and the open meadow beyond. The last of the lightning bugs flickered and danced in the soft, blurry darkness. Daddy's prize plantation pacers whinnied softly from the barn as Hector locked them in for the night.

"Well," Mama said quietly, "it's certainly something to consider. Boarding Union officers. But I can't make a decision without Gaylen."

"And how do you think you'll get his advice, Vashti?" Mrs. Campbell's knitting needles clicked furiously. "You know as well as I that General Lyon has cut off all the roads out of town. No one can get a message across Union lines now."

"Mrs. Campbell's right, Mama," I said, thinking of Daddy's study filled with books, his plantation pacing horses, the ripening cornfields on our farm south of town. "The last thing Daddy would want us to do is lose our home. We have to fight for it any way we can."

Mrs. Phelps reached into her basket and pulled out a piece of paper. She unfolded it slowly. "I took the liberty today to speak to Mr. Phelps about this very matter," she said, pausing to look at Mama. "There's an officer—and his wife—who just arrived yesterday afternoon and have yet to find a suitable situation." She handed the paper to Mama.

"What do you know of this Captain and Mrs. Brown?" Mama asked.

"He's from New York, an army regular. She's an English-woman. Mr. Phelps says she's very genteel."

Mama still stared at the paper. Before she could give a reply, we all heard the sounds of soldiers out front: horses snorting, boots on the front porch, a knock at the door.

Was this how it had happened at the Grimeses?

Juneau glided through the back door. "Soldiers here to see you, Miz Vashti."

"I will have no discourse with the enemy," Mama said, her voice steady.

"That's not wise, Vashti." Mrs. Phelps's hoop skirts rustled as she got to her feet.

"Then tell them I am not at home," Mama answered.

Mrs. Phelps and Mrs. Campbell exchanged glances. "Let me see what I can do," Mrs. Phelps said softly.

Mama nodded and motioned for me to join Mrs. Phelps. "Keep your wits about you, Reeves," she whispered, "and stall for time."

I followed Mrs. Phelps and Juneau down the hall to the front door, where a tall Federal officer stood with his back to us. He turned suddenly.

Percival Wilder.

Mrs. Phelps held out her hand. "So good to see you again, Percy. You don't mind if I still call you Percy now that you're an important aide-de-camp to General Lyon."

He bowed and smiled. "Not at all. But I'm here to see Mrs. O'Neill." He glanced down the front hall.

I stepped in front of Juneau. "My mother is . . . indisposed. Perhaps I can help you."

"I'm here on official business."

"Like this afternoon at the Grimeses?" I stared straight into his deep brown eyes.

Percival Wilder winced. But then he should have.

Mrs. Phelps glanced at me, then edged closer to Lieutenant Wilder. "Surely this can wait until morning, Percy. It's getting late."

The door opened wider, revealing a dozen soldiers clustered around the front porch. Their firearms gleamed in the light that spilled from the doorway. Juneau put her hands on my shoulders. They felt firm and strong.

Percival Wilder reached into his breast pocket and pulled out a piece of paper. He unfolded it slowly and handed it to Mrs. Phelps.

She read it swiftly, then gave it to me. "It's a requisition, Reeves. For fifteen head of your daddy's horses."

"General Lyon has authorized a payment in army scrip," explained Lieutenant Wilder. "It's the best we can do right now, Miss O'Neill."

"You will be paid, Reeves," Mrs. Phelps said. "This isn't a confiscation."

"But you're taking fifteen of my daddy's horses, and they're not for sale."

"This is war, Miss O'Neill. The army needs them."

Juneau's hands pressed more firmly against my shoulders. "Hush, Miz Reeves," she whispered. "Let Mizzus Phelps take care of this."

Mrs. Phelps took the requisition from my hands and

folded it into her pocket. "I'll send Mr. Phelps over tomorrow, and he can advise Reeves on which horses the army needs. It's too dark to examine the horses right now, anyway. Surely you can agree to that, Percy?"

He paused, then looked at me.

"All right. But tomorrow morning at nine o'clock."

"Good." Mrs. Phelps turned. "Come, Reeves. It's getting late, and I'm sure these good men need to return to their camp. Good night, Percy."

Mrs. Phelps turned and led Juneau down the hall toward the back porch. I waited for Percival Wilder to leave, but he lingered in the doorway. As soon as we heard the back door click shut, he took my arm.

"Don't touch me." I yanked away.

"I just wanted to explain." His face was flushed, his eyes dark. "My men got out of hand today. They're hungry and poorly clothed. Our supplies haven't come through from St. Louis, and—"

"And that's your excuse for stealing from innocent people," I snapped. "Just because they happen to believe in something you and your men don't."

He leaned close. I could feel his breath warm against my cheek. "If your mother doesn't take the oath or seek the protection of Federal officers, it will happen to you, too. I guarantee it."

CHAPTER 7

I never thought that I would be susceptible to the stir-rings of romance, especially now when the whole world lurches and spins like a broken top. Yet today when Lieutenant Percival Wilder took my hand, it felt as if a tiny cluster of honeybees were swarming around my heart. But he is the enemy. What if he were to fire at Daddy, and Daddy were to fire back?

—The Diary of Margaret Reeves O'Neill,
August 1, 1861

"WE COULD HIDE Mr. Gaylen's best horses down at the old dairy barn," Hector suggested the next morning before day-break. "Herd them down through Mrs. Campbell's fields to the south farm without crossing any of the main roads. General Lyon's soldiers will be none the wiser."

Well, you could have knocked me down with a feather! But I knew Hector suggested it because he loved Daddy's horses better than he loved almost anything. Hector and I had learned to ride together when we were children, and last year Daddy had made Hector a gift of Titania, a blood bay filly with fire in her eyes.

"He'll be off to Kansas or Indian Territory before you can say Jack Robinson," Mama had warned.

"Maybe," Daddy had replied. "And maybe not. Hector has a way with horses. I'd like to train him to run the business—if something ever happens to me."

And that had silenced Mama—for the moment.

So by six o'clock, Hector and Bruno, the foreman on our south farm, had herded nine of Daddy's best and favorite horses—Mama's mare Esmie, Slippers and her foal, Jefferson and all the rest—down past the pond and across the open field toward the Campbells'. I rode with them until we cleared the cedars on our property line.

Hector reined in Titania and looked out across the Campbells' corn fields, corn so high it could hide a horse and rider. A nagging little fear popped into my mind, like a wispy cloud in a cloudless sky. Was Hector planning to run away and take our horses with him? Could I trust him?

He turned and smiled. "Most of the soldiers I've seen so far wouldn't know a horse from a heifer."

I tried to meet Hector's eyes, but he wouldn't look me square in the face. Still, I had no choice: I had to trust him.

"Ride as fast as you can, Hector," I said. "I'll need you back at the house to show the horses to Lieutenant Wilder."

He stared right through me, then dug his boots into his filly's flanks. Bruno tipped his hat in my general direction and followed. I watched until the corn swallowed them up.

"I TELL YOU, Mrs. O'Neill, you have to cooperate with these men. They mean business." Congressman Phelps's voice came from the study.

I closed the front door behind me and pulled off my riding gloves. Softly, I walked down the hall, waiting for Mama's response.

"You and Mary are good friends to me, Congressman, though it pains me to see you take the Union side in this," she said. "You stand to lose significant property yourselves if Mr. Lincoln were to emancipate all our people."

"I'm fighting for the Union, and if the time comes to emancipate our negroes, I've been assured that President Lincoln will recommend full compensation for our losses." Mr. Phelps paused. "But you and your girls, Mrs. O'Neill, you could lose everything you own, right this very minute."

I stopped just outside the doorway.

At last Mama said, "You're right, of course. I must do whatever will keep home and hearth together."

"Then you'll welcome your guests this afternoon?" Mr. Phelps asked.

"Yes," Mama said softly. "Captain and Mrs. Brown."

I cleared my throat and stepped across the threshold.

"Here, at last!" Mama crossed the room and drew me toward Congressman Phelps. "I'm afraid you'll have to talk to Reeves about our horses. I declare sometimes she knows more about my husband's business affairs than I do." Then Mama laughed a bitter little laugh, the one she had used at the supper table when Daddy talked about his will. She left me alone with Mr. Phelps.

*   *   *

WE WALKED down the long row of stalls. If he noticed more were empty than usual, he didn't say anything. At the far end of the barn, the congressman turned and unfolded the requisition.

"Fifteen horses. And you have eighteen here, plus the carriage horses. I suggest that you let the lieutenant make his own choices. But he may take the whole lot of them."

Percival Wilder and his men arrived an hour later. He saluted Congressman Phelps but wouldn't look at me, which was fine. I had nothing to say to him either.

"Miss Reeves will act on behalf of her mother in this matter," Congressman Phelps explained as we walked back down to the barn. "I've already looked at the horses, and everything seems in order. Still . . ."

He paused, and I held my breath. I knew Mr. Phelps knew we had more than eighteen horses on the place.

"Still, I didn't see that negro boy who manages the stables for Mr. O'Neill." He stopped and looked at me. "Where is he, Reeves? I'm sure Lieutenant Wilder would like to consult him before making any choices."

Before I could answer, Hector walked out of the horse barn, his shirt drenched with sweat. He'd ridden hard to get back so soon. I nodded to him, and this time he looked me square in the eye. He'd done me a great favor, and we both knew it.

"Just got back from the Campbells' south farm, " Hector fibbed, his accent exaggerated for the lieutenant's benefit. "Little Miz Lucy had a hankerin' for that fine, white sweet

corn the Campbell boys grow down toward Wilson's Creek."
He wiped his hands on his overalls. "Reckon you'll have it
for lunch, Miz Reeves."

"Thank you, Hector," I said, wondering suddenly what
Hector would expect in return for his favor and his cool little
lie. I kept my voice steady and tried to sound like Mama,
when she told one of our people what to do. "Now, I need
you to show Lieutenant Wilder here our livestock. I'm sure
he has other business to attend to this morning."

I glanced at the lieutenant coldly, and he brushed past me,
tall and straight and steady. Then I followed him and Congressman Phelps into the barn.

We were there for nearly an hour. The lieutenant in-
spected each horse slowly, thoroughly. He'd run his hand
along a horse's neck, then across its back and rump, talking
to it softly, checking its legs and hooves.

"He's one soldier who knows a horse from a heifer," Hector whispered. Indeed, Lieutenant Wilder's knowledge was
impressive, for he recognized the strengths, and the weak-
nesses, in every single horse he examined.

"Your father runs a fine stable, Miss O'Neill," he said at
last.

Then we walked down between the stalls and he made his
choices. With each one, I felt another piece of Daddy slip-
ping away. But I held my head up high and forced back the
tears I knew I'd cry later on.

"I'll leave you these three," Percival Wilder continued.
"The yearling, the mare, and the gelding, as well as your

carriage horses. Though the time may come when the army will need even these."

He signed the requisition, then passed it to me for my signature. Mr. Phelps served as witness.

"I'll take this to headquarters and exchange it for scrip if you like, Reeves," Mr. Phelps said softly, his arm on my shoulder.

"That would be a great kindness." I tried to smile, but couldn't.

A swarm of soldiers suddenly appeared in the doorway to lead Daddy's horses away. Hector's eyes had filled with tears. I didn't know he could cry. But I knew if I didn't get away fast, I'd be crying myself. There. In front of Percival Wilder and all his soldiers. I turned away and walked out toward the pond just as fast as my hoops would let me. Away from Daddy's horses, away from horses the enemy would use against him. Tears burned my eyes, spilled down my face. I didn't know Lieutenant Wilder had followed me until it was too late.

"I had been led to believe your father's operation here was somewhat bigger," he said.

He was right behind me. "Do you want to look at Daddy's books?" I asked, hoping that he wouldn't, brushing my tears away.

"No, Miss O'Neill. But please turn around. I have something important to say."

"What more can you possibly have to say to me?" I hoped my voice sounded cold and hateful. "You've taken what you came for."

He thrust a piece of paper over my shoulder. "Here are the names of two highly esteemed officers who need housing immediately. If you could persuade your mother to accept them, then your family will have the protection it needs . . ." He paused. "No matter where your true sympathies lie."

"Is one of the names your own?" I asked.

"No, I already have acceptable quarters." He looked away, back toward the porch where Lucy and Little Lou Campbell were drinking lemonade and fanning themselves with a pair of Mama's fine Japanese fans. Finally he said, "It's just that I won't be able to keep an eye on your family for a few days. I'm riding out in the morning with General Lyon. We hope to engage General Price's troops in battle."

I almost said, "If you're going to fight my daddy, why worry about us?" But instead, I turned slowly. "You don't have to worry about us anymore, Lieutenant Wilder. Congressman and Mrs. Phelps have already arranged for an officer and his wife to come live with us today. Captain and Mrs. Brown."

Percival Wilder stared at me for what seemed like an eternity. Finally, he said, "Captain and Mrs. Horatio Brown?"

He leaned closer.

My cheeks felt warm, my legs unsteady. It was a most provoking feeling, and I didn't like it one bit. So I took a step back.

"I know only that their name is Brown."

"Tiger Eye," he whispered to himself. "Tiger Eye Brown." Then he took my hand so firmly that I couldn't pull it back, and before I rightly knew what was happening, he'd kissed it.

"Take care, Miss O'Neill," he murmured. "Very great care."

I stood there all atremble as he walked away. What a traitor I'd become, accepting the advances of my enemy.

CHAPTER 8

Now we share our home with the enemy—a Captain
and Mrs. Brown. She disapproves of Percival Wilder as
strongly as Mama. In whom should I believe? Still, I
kindle the hope that Mrs. Brown will become my friend.
For she is a published poetess.

— The Diary of Margaret Reeves O'Neill,
August 1, 1861

THAT VERY AFTERNOON, Mrs. Horatio Brown swept through
our front door in an elaborate traveling costume of pale lavender and apple green that made Mama's fine blue muslin look
like a hand-me-down.

"What a charming home, my dear Mrs. O'Neill, and so generous of you to share it with those who fight for what is right."

Her crisp British accent was bright and cheerful, but her
colorless eyes narrowed. And I couldn't help but wonder if
she knew all about us, including the fact that Daddy was
fighting for the other side.

Mama's reply was chilly. "Welcome to our home. May
your stay be comfortable, and as brief as we all hope this war
shall be."

"It'll be brief all right!" Captain Brown edged around his
wife's skirts and twirled his silky moustache. He must have
been at least four inches shorter than Mrs. Brown, despite

the high-heeled riding boots that distinguished his uniform. He took Mama's hand and bowed. "We'll whip those lawless rebels and send them packing."

Mama blanched. It wasn't going to be easy living side by side with Daddy's enemies.

At just that moment, Hector and Bruno staggered through the front door with a massive steamer trunk, the biggest I'd ever seen. Juneau slipped in from the kitchen and pointed to Mama's good China rug.

"Over there, Hector. Don't mar Miz Vashti's walnut floors," she ordered, pulling Lucy out of the way.

"Looks like we done been invaded, Miz Vashti," Bruno whispered, dodging Mrs. Brown's hoops as he headed for the door and yet another trunk.

"Please don't be alarmed by all this," Mrs. Brown said sweetly, gesturing toward the trunks. "They're books, mostly. I travel with a complete library, especially when Horatio's duties take us west, to what might be uncivilized territory."

Mama bristled at the word *uncivilized,* but I took hope. If we had to open our doors to Daddy's enemies, wouldn't it be easier if they shared his passion for literature?

"Do check, Horatio," Mrs. Brown continued, "and make sure everything has arrived undamaged."

Captain Brown unlocked the first trunk, and I edged closer, hoping to recognize my favorite titles among Mrs. Brown's collection. Indeed, I was not disappointed. Chaucer. Shakespeare. The Romantic poets.

"Everything seems to be in order, my darling," Captain Brown said.

Hector edged nearer and bent to examine the books.

"Unload them later, boy," Mrs. Brown said lightly, taking a book from Hector's hand. His eyes glared, but he backed away, obedient as Juneau had always taught him to be. Then Captain Brown took out a stack of newspaper clippings tied with a scarlet ribbon. He handed them to Mrs. Brown. "Your literary master works, my sweeting." He turned back to Mama. "My wife is a published poetess, you know."

"A poetess!" Lucy gasped with delight.

My own heart began to race.

"Yes, and a fine poetess she is, young lady." Captain Brown chucked Lucy under the chin, then got to his feet—a bit unsteadily because the heels of his boots wobbled a little.

"Reeves writes poetry sometimes," Lucy gushed. "Stories, too."

I felt a blush steal across my face.

Mrs. Brown tapped the packet of clippings against her arm and strolled toward Lucy and me. "And who, pray tell, is Reeves?"

Mama pushed me forward ever so slightly. "Margaret Reeves, my elder daughter. It might surprise you to learn, Mrs. Brown, that in this wild, uncivilized country of ours, a young lady could entertain such ambitions. But my husband is very learned and feels she shows great promise."

I knew my face had turned as red as hot coals. Since when did Mama take pride in my writing—and in front of a published poetess! But I met Mrs. Brown's steady gaze and made a deep curtsy, my mind racing for something to say, something to turn the conversation away from me. So I blurted out, "I believe we have a mutual acquaintance, Mrs. Brown."

"And who might that be, my dear?"

I paused, knowing Mama wouldn't like my answer, then plunged ahead anyway. "A Lieutenant Percival Wilder, from St. Louis."

Mama frowned. So did Mrs. Brown. "What did he tell you about me?" she asked, her eyes suddenly narrow and cold, making me feel as if I'd said something highly improper.

Before I could stammer out a reply, Mrs. Brown tilted my chin with her fingertip. "Please accept a word of advice, Miss O'Neill. Beware casual acquaintances during times of war. It is so easy to be misled or to accept an untruth from those who practice deceit when times are tumultuous. Do you not agree, Mrs. O'Neill?"

Mama said nothing.

The spot on my right hand where Percival Wilder's lips had brushed against my glove positively burned.

"I fear," Mrs. Brown continued, "that among the better circles of St. Louis society, young Percival Wilder's conduct is thought to be scandalous."

Oh, my skin was on fire! And I could feel Mama's gaze upon me, heavy as a wool blanket in summertime. But was Percival Wilder truly scandalous? Whom should I believe?

"You know the Wilders, then?" Lucy persisted, for she loved to hear grown-up gossip.

"Know them? I'll say Miranda knows them!" Captain Brown shook his head. "The old man himself must have rejected her poetry hundreds of times. But he cut off his nose to spite his face." He pointed to the clippings Mrs. Brown held in her hand. "You've probably read my wife's poetry in all the papers, even *Frank Leslie's Illustrated.*"

Now Mrs. Brown flushed, though from embarrassment or anger I couldn't tell. But I did believe that *The Wilder Review* set higher poetic standards than *Frank Leslie's Illustrated Newspaper.*

Then an awkward silence descended like a cold morning fog. For once even Mama didn't have a proverb or old saying on the tip of her tongue to smooth over an uncomfortable situation. Finally, Captain Brown cleared his throat and turned abruptly toward his wife.

"I must be off to the front, my darling. Give me a kiss." He stood on tiptoe to reach Mrs. Brown's face, and his lips brushed her cheek lightly.

What an unsatisfactory way to say good-bye. For I remembered Daddy, sweeping Mama in his arms, kissing her right on the mouth.

But I was even more surprised when Mrs. Brown turned away from the door. She didn't watch Captain Brown ride away, though she had to know it might be the last time she'd see him alive. After all, if Percival Wilder had told the truth, the whole Federal army was going into combat the very next day—against General Price . . . and Daddy.

Instead, Mrs. Brown turned to Mama.

"There are a few things I'll need right away," she said, unpinning her hat and handing it to Juneau, as if it were the most natural thing in the world for Juneau to wait on her.

"Miz Vashti's furnished your room as if it were her own," Juneau said flatly, holding Mrs. Brown's Empress Eugénie hat at arm's length like a dead possum.

"Still, none of you knew I was a poetess and, therefore, would need a suitable place to ply my pen." Mrs. Brown paused, then flashed a smile in my direction. "Perhaps that brilliant father of yours, Miss Margaret Reeves, is also a writer and has a library that would furnish my needs perfectly."

"Why, it's right down the hall and—"

I slapped my hand over Lucy's mouth. For no matter how grand a poetess Mrs. Brown might be, Daddy's study was his very own. That wide mahogany desk, the rows of books, the high windows . . .

But then Mama said, "We have just the thing for a poetess like you, Mrs. Brown." Mama glanced in my direction, and I feared, suddenly, that only I knew just how much Daddy's study had meant to him. "We'll move Reeves's writing desk into your room later this afternoon."

I started to protest, but Mama held up her hand. "Show Mrs. Brown to her room, Juneau."

"Thank you, Mrs. O'Neill," Mrs. Brown replied in a dull, unhappy voice. I watched as she followed Juneau upstairs. Surely Mama could have fulfilled Mrs. Brown's request some other way.

Then she folded me in her arms. "Clean out your desk, Margaret Reeves, and move everything into your Daddy's study." Mama pressed the key into my hand. "It's yours now, until he comes home."

CHAPTER 9

Enclosed herein please find my latest scrap of poesy, "The Icy Hand of Death." It is a poem in twelve stanzas depicting the pitiful plight of a runaway slave.

    —Mrs. Horatio Brown to *Frank Leslie's*
      Illustrated, August 2, 1861

I AWOKE IN THE DARK of the night to the muffled sounds of horses and wagons and men. I glanced across at Lucy, who was sleeping peacefully, then tiptoed to the window. Under a bright August moon, Jefferson Street was packed with soldiers, marching south.

So Percival Wilder had spoken the truth! General Lyon and his Federal army were marching to war. For an instant, I felt a pure rush of joy, a renewed confidence in the character of Lieutenant Wilder.

But what was I thinking?

No matter how noble his character, Lieutenant Wilder was my daddy's enemy, and by rights, he should have been mine as well. I turned away from the window, an unspeakable heaviness in my heart.

Then I thought of Mrs. Brown. How great must her sorrow be, knowing her husband was on the road to war. Was she standing at her window, searching the shadowy faces for one last glimpse of the man she loved?

THE NEXT morning, Lucy's bed was empty, but her laughter floated down the hall like a robin's song at dawn. I threw on my wrapper and followed the sound of Lucy's voice. There she was, curled up on Mrs. Brown's bed, a pencil stuck behind her ear.

"My dear Lucy," Mrs. Brown was saying, the rosy glow of a good night's sleep upon her cheeks, "a rhymed couplet must always rhyme. Perhaps you should use my rhyming dictionary."

Daddy had always scorned such tools. "A writer should have a natural ear for language," he'd say. But perhaps Lucy had forgotten. She laughed. "I do so want to be a poetess, Mrs. Brown. Just like you."

Mrs. Brown nodded graciously and handed Lucy the dictionary. It was a thick, battered volume, so well used that most of its red binding had peeled away.

"Reeves," Lucy gushed, "Mrs. Brown's promised to make me a great poetess. I've just this minute decided that's what I want to be." She giggled and scrunched deeper into Mrs. Brown's feather pillows. "Won't Daddy be proud?"

I tried to smile back, watching Lucy thumb through the dictionary. Her writing had always been impossible.

"What rhymes with *lavender*?" Lucy frowned. "*Pavender. Cavender. Scavenger*! And I didn't even use the dictionary!" She smiled radiantly—first at me, then at Mrs. Brown.

"Won't you join us, Miss Margaret Reeves?" Mrs. Brown crooned. "Lucy has kindly given me your portfolio to read, and I'm eager to discuss it with you."

"You—you did *what?*" I sputtered at Lucy.

"Oh, I knew you'd be too shy to show it to anyone." Lucy beamed. "But here it is." She held up my slim, leather writing portfolio, the one that contained the final copies of what Daddy thought were my very best stories.

"If you prefer, we could always examine your work later," Mrs. Brown suggested. "I only desire to be of service."

I was too stunned to object. Then Cook called us to breakfast, and Mrs. Brown glided downstairs.

"Do let her read your stories, Reeves," Lucy pleaded. "She's promised to give us both writing lessons." Her eyes were so eager, so full of the same hope I nourished in my own heart, that I had to agree.

MRS. BROWN made another surprising suggestion that morning at breakfast. "Have you ever given thought to having your photographs made, Mrs. O'Neill?" she asked as Juneau poured her a second cup of coffee. "Your daughters are beauties," she said, turning her smile on Mama, "and it's clear to see from whence their beauty came."

Lucy glanced at Mama hopefully. We'd none of us ever had our portraits made by a photographer. But Mama was unmoved by Mrs. Brown's flattery. "This hardly seems the time for portraiture, Mrs. Brown. The entire country is waiting for war." She stirred the cream in her coffee so violently that it spilled into the saucer.

Mrs. Brown swept out of her chair and clutched her hand to her heart. "I daresay this does not apply to you," she said, "but many families are sending photographs to their loved ones, serving in the heat of battle. I know my dear Horatio is marching off to war this very instant, bearing such an image of me next to his heart." Her gaze turned soft and misty. For the first time, she displayed genuine affection for her husband.

Mama stopped stirring her coffee, and I knew that she was thinking of Daddy, so far away, marching against the Federal army, against Mrs. Brown's Horatio. Her eyes filled with sudden tears, and her face flushed cherub pink.

"Forgive me, Mrs. O'Neill," Mrs. Brown said sweetly, seeing Mama's distress. "I forgot that your husband has apparently chosen not to serve in the military. . . ." She paused. "Where did you say he has gone?"

She sounded innocent enough, but the question she posed was an indelicate, even dangerous, one. We could lose everything if we openly admitted Daddy was with General Price. Mama quickly wiped away her tears. Lucy's face went scarlet, and I feared she'd blurt out the truth. So I said, as cool as you please, "Daddy's tending to business in Ohio."

"What an inconvenient time for a man to engage in business," she replied, staring so boldly across the table at me that I knew she didn't believe my story for an instant. My mind raced ahead, trying to create a series of believable details to answer the questions I thought Mrs. Brown was about to raise, when suddenly she smiled, all sunshine and rainbows.

"Truly," she said, "it matters little how a man occupies his time. If he is far away, I'm sure he would appreciate a portrait of his family."

Almost, I could have believed that I'd misinterpreted Mrs. Brown's entire manner, but one look at Mama told me that she, too, shared my apprehensions. Only Lucy seemed unfazed.

"I think she's right," Lucy ventured. "With Daddy so far away in *Ohio* on *business,* I'm sure he'd like a picture of us all." Lucy sparkled, proud that she'd kept a cool head after all. "We could send it by mail."

"But there isn't any mail, Lucy," I said flatly.

"I'm sure we could find a way to reach your father, darling," Mrs. Brown cooed. "I'll consult Horatio when he returns."

"Please, Mama. May we?" Lucy begged.

Mama frowned and walked away from the table. She stood at the window, watching Old Peter pinching back the marigolds. When she finally spoke, her words came soft and low.

"I will consider it, Mrs. Brown. Perhaps it would provide a measure of comfort to my beloved so far away from us."

EARLY THAT afternoon, I found myself standing outside Mrs. Brown's doorway, trying to summon up the courage to speak to her about my portfolio. I was as trembly as a newborn colt testing its legs. Truly, had Lucy not taken my portfolio in hand, I wouldn't have thought of imposing on Mrs. Brown in this manner.

But, as much as I longed for her guidance, my heart was not completely at ease. There was something about Mrs. Brown that did not inspire confidence: her indiscreet questioning about Daddy's whereabouts, her assessment of Percival Wilder's character. Still, I told myself, her interest in my writing seemed genuine. Perhaps the temper of the times had so biased my powers of observation that I saw duplicity where none was intended.

I took a deep breath and knocked softly on her bedroom door, then knocked again. When no one answered, I pushed it open. Mrs. Brown stood with her back to me, a manuscript in her hands. She read in a fine, deep, dramatic voice:

> *"Into the turbulent whirl*
> *Did the frenzied woman swirl,*
> *And the icy hand of death*
> *To the troubled soul, gave rest."*

Lucy broke into wild applause. "What do you think of Mrs. Brown's poem, Reeves? Isn't it grand?"

I couldn't help but wonder if Mrs. Brown had relied on her rhyming dictionary for such a work. But then, I'd heard only four lines. So I smiled and complimented Mrs. Brown as best I could. "Your reading certainly heightens the poem's drama."

"Thank you," she said briskly. "And now, for your port-folio." She placed it under her arm and waltzed toward my writing desk. "Nothing pleases me more than the opportu-nity to tutor a pair of aspiring young writers."

Mrs. Brown's voice was smooth, but it made me feel small somehow and unimportant, as if there were nothing in all the world so insignificant as an aspiring young writer. Once again, I felt unsure of her of real intentions.

Reluctantly I perched on the edge of her featherbed, watching as she sat at my writing desk and sorted through first one story, then another. Lucy read over Mrs. Brown's shoulder. Why did that irritate me so? The minutes passed ever so slowly, and with each turning of a page, I felt a fear-some tightening in my chest that felt like the grippe. Her silence was agony.

And then I realized that I'd made a horrible mistake, that stuffed in the middle of my portfolio was "The Happy Pic-nickers," that flimsy tale that Daddy had deemed unworthy on our last morning together. I edged closer to Mrs. Brown and recognized the opening sentence to the story. *"Off to the little church in the glade they went, hampers brimming with the fruits of summer."* My face went hot as a cookstove, my arms as limp as overripe rhubarb. I couldn't have snatched back that story if my life depended on it.

Suddenly Mrs. Brown snapped the folder shut and stared at me a moment. Lucy waited breathlessly for Mrs. Brown's verdict.

"Well, Margaret Reeves," Mrs. Brown said at last. "We have our work cut out for us, don't we?" She handed me the portfolio, and I felt as if all the life in my body had been sucked away.

She began to pace across the room, and her high-heeled slippers tapped against the floor like rifle fire. "Your writing lacks sentiment and emotion, a certain dramatic quality that tells the reader what to think and how to feel. You must leave nothing to the reader's imagination."

Everything she said contradicted what I'd learned from Daddy!

"Only one story here approaches anything even remotely publishable," Mrs. Brown continued. "This one about the picnic. It's your best."

"But Daddy didn't think so!" Lucy gasped.

"Remember, dear Lucy, that I am a published poetess." Mrs. Brown's accent was clipped, confident. "Your daddy is simply an amateur."

A cold wave of contempt spread through my veins like a bitter tonic. How dare she insult Daddy so? He was a fine critic. What did it matter if he had never published poetry in *Frank Leslie's Illustrated*?

"Give me your story, Margaret Reeves, and I will edit it for you," Mrs. Brown demanded, her hands outstretched. "Inexperienced young writers often lack critical insight, especially when poorly tutored in their formative years."

I clutched my portfolio even tighter. Never, never, would I betray Daddy's lessons to me. "No thank you, Mrs. Brown," I said, trembling with anger and heartache. "I can do that myself."

CHAPTER 10

*My hostess and her preening daughters today have had
their images forever captured by the photographer's craft.
They scheme to send their pitiful portraits south, to a
traitorous father, who even now may be leveling his rifle
sights on one of our own Noble Fighting Men of this
Glorious Union.*

—Tiger Eye, Special Dispatch
to *The Cincinnati Commercial*,
August 3, 1861

AT BREAKFAST the next morning, I avoided conversation
with Mrs. Brown, but she and Lucy chattered away about all
kinds of subjects—the width of hoop skirts in Paris, the
proper age at which a young lady may accept the attentions of
a suitor, how to eat fried chicken without using one's fingers.

Mama didn't say a word. Finally, just as Juneau was pouring out our last cups of coffee, Mama made an announce-
ment: The three of us would have our picture taken that very
afternoon.

"You'll never regret this decision!" Mrs. Brown exclaimed.

Mama merely nodded, then turned to me. "Send Hector
on down to the square, Margaret Reeves," she ordered, "and
have him secure us an appointment with the photographer."

I found Hector in Daddy's horse barn, empty now except for the three plantation pacers Percival Wilder had spared us, a pair of mules, and the carriage horses. I delivered Mama's message, and Hector led one of the mules from its stall.

"Have you any news from Bruno?" I asked as Hector reached for a bridle.

"All Mr. Gaylen's horses are accounted for," he said. "There's been no trouble from any soldiers." He paused. "But you might want to take a look at that." He nodded toward a newspaper, folded on the low bench by the doorway.

I scooped up the paper. "Why wasn't this delivered to the house?"

Hector forced the bit into the mule's mouth. "My mama didn't think you'd miss it." He paused again. "To tell the truth, she's been bringing me the paper ever since Mr. Gaylen left for Cowskin Prairie. It's all I've had to read since he's been gone."

"I see."

I sank onto the bench and stared down at my sleek, black boots. Truly, I hadn't seen a *Springfield Journal* in weeks, but then it was being published so sporadically because of the Federal occupation that I hadn't even missed it. Still, I should have been alarmed by this little deception. After all, as Mama liked to say, one's people shouldn't put their own concerns ahead of their masters'. But Daddy himself had taught Hector how to read, so I tried to respond as he might have done by saying, "In the future, if you want something to read, why don't you just ask?"

Hector shrugged. Then he threw a saddle across the mule's back and reached for the cinch. "Turn to the inside front page, Miss Reeves," he said. "The story by the correspondent from *The Cincinnati Commercial*."

I skimmed the first paragraph:

I now live among Rebels—a family of self-satisfied, slave-holding women, with the trappings of culture and the sensibilities of scullery maids.

An uncomfortable, jittery feeling settled into the pit of my stomach, but I read on.

The correspondent described a Springfield family, a mother, two girls, and their household servants—the housekeeper and her son, the cook, an old gardener. It might have been us—or it might not. The characters in this correspondent's account went unnamed, and their personal attributes were as highly exaggerated as anything Mrs. Stowe had written in *Uncle Tom's Cabin*. I skipped down to the last paragraph.

I promise my readers more insight into the workings of a Rebel family, and the tangled web they have woven that is called Slavery.

The story was signed *Tiger Eye*.

Hector led the mule through the door, out into the hot August sunshine. Then he turned. "Interesting, isn't it?"

I swallowed hard. "Yes. It certainly is." *But surely, surely it's not about us,* a voice inside me screamed. *For who could write such things about us?*

Truly, I was afraid of the answer.

Then Hector swung into the saddle and headed for the photographer's.

LATER THAT afternoon, I avoided Hector's gaze as he handed me into the carriage. Why had he shown me that article? Did he suspect Mrs. Brown?

"Margaret Reeves, pay attention," Mama snapped, snatching my skirt back as Hector closed the carriage door. "For once, do try to concentrate on your appearance." Mama's face was pinched with worry. "What will the photographer think if we arrive in disarray?"

Lucy adjusted her hair ribbons as Juneau settled Mama's carpetbag of beauty supplies on her lap.

"Let's go, Hector," Mama ordered.

"Good-bye, my dears!" Mrs. Brown called from the front porch. "You all look heavenly!"

It was hotter than a baker's oven sitting inside the enclosed carriage, but Mama had insisted on it. "We must protect ourselves from the dust of the road," she'd said. "No telling what imperfections that photographer's camera might detect."

We weren't two blocks from home when Mama herself detected an imperfection. "Margaret Reeves O'Neill, is that India ink on your Spanish lace?"

Indeed, it was—just a tiny, tiny smear.

Lucy giggled. Mama sighed and shook her head. "Did we bring a suitable substitute, Juneau?"

Juneau rummaged through Mama's carpetbag and draped three pieces of lace across her arm. "They're all skimpy, Miz Vashti. Not enough yardage to fill in around Miz Reeves's throat."

Mama sighed again. "Stop the carriage, Hector. We'll have to turn around, though we're already so behind our time that I don't know how the photographer will be able to work us in." Mama's lips trembled, and I could tell she was genuinely grieved.

So I said, "You go on ahead, Mama. I'll walk back to the house and change my lace. Then Old Peter can drive me to the square."

"But your dress!" Lucy cried. "It'll be soiled!"

"I'll brush if off at home and wear a duster on the way back."

Mama's eyes brightened. "Well, perhaps all is not lost after all." She paused. "But be quick about it, Margaret Reeves. Remember, a young lady should be punctual in all her appointments."

I SLIPPED upstairs and found a fine lace fluff in Mama's upper right bureau drawer. But before I could secure it properly around my neck, the back stairs creaked as if someone were sneaking out by way of the kitchen. I tiptoed down the hall and looked around the corner. Downstairs, the hem of Mrs. Brown's wide, plaid skirt swirled across the kitchen floor toward the door. By the time I got to the kitchen, she was standing in the backyard.

"You there!" I heard her command. "Saddle me a horse right away."

"Yes 'um, Miz Brown."

I recognized Old Peter's voice and watched from the kitchen window as Mrs. Brown followed him to the horse barn. When they returned, Old Peter was leading Ivanhoe, the slowest, steadiest pacer we owned. As he helped Mrs. Brown into the saddle, I laced on a sturdy pair of boots Juneau kept by the kitchen door and dashed toward the redbud grove. Something told me Mrs. Brown needed watching.

I FOLLOWED Mrs. Brown on foot, keeping my distance because the streets were empty—not a single soldier in sight. She rode straight for the square, glanced at Mama's empty carriage by the photographer's, then reined in Ivanhoe at the Western Union office. I followed as close as I dared but hung back in the deep, shady doorway of Coleman's Store. Still, I could hear her voice as clearly as if we were standing in the same room.

"For *The Cincinnati Commercial*," she ordered. "Right away."

That queer, unsettled feeling in my stomach returned.

"But, Ma'am," I heard the clerk protest, "this here message is too dad-blamed long. It'll cost ya a small fortune."

"My editor pays his bills. Now, hurry up."

A dozen riders kicked up a cloud of dust on the opposite side of the square. They rode fast and hard, Federal soldiers in distinctive blue-and-gray uniforms, blazing past the Western Union, around the corner, down toward Federal headquarters. Were they bringing back war news?

Quickly I consulted my notebook tucked into the pocket of my dusty watered silk. According to my notes, they wore the uniforms of the quartermaster's requisition staff. They'd have no news from the front.

But no one else seemed to know that, and suddenly the square was choked with people hungry for news, hungry for war. Mrs. Brown and the Western Union clerk dashed outside and joined the throng rushing behind the soldiers. I stole inside. Mrs. Brown's message rested on the counter.

Now it is true that I was raised better than to read other people's correspondence, and under any other circumstance I wouldn't have dared. But that afternoon I couldn't help myself. And I had only to read the first line to confirm my worst fears: *"My hostess and her preening daughters today have had their images forever captured by the photographer's craft."*

Words and phrases burned my eyes as surely as hot coals. *"Pitiful portraits." "Traitorous father."* Mrs. Brown's handwriting looped across the page, filling every space with half-truths and lies. We were ourselves—and we weren't.

Then I saw her signature, scrawled across the bottom of the last page.

Tiger Eye.

Suddenly I knew where I'd heard that name before. I could hear Percival Wilder's low whisper, feel the touch of his hand, the memory was so strong. *"Tiger Eye. Tiger Eye Brown."*

I snatched up the dispatch and raced outside, back down St. Louis Street, across Jefferson, all the way home. For the moment, I forgot all about Mama and Lucy, waiting for me across the square.

"HOW DARE YOU, Margaret Reeves O'Neill! How dare you forget an obligation to your family!" Mama's face was scarlet with rage.

"We had our pictures taken anyway! Without you!" Lucy's face was streaked with tears. "You're going to break Daddy's heart!" Then she stormed upstairs and slammed our bedroom door behind her.

I followed Mama into the parlor. "Read this," I whispered, pressing Tiger Eye's dispatch into Mama's hands. "Read it now."

Mama paced to the window, so I couldn't see her face. But moments later, I knew exactly what she was feeling. "That scheming piece of British baggage!" She crumpled the dispatch in her hand and turned back toward me. Her skirt swooped out, knocking over the rosewood side table. A hand-painted tray shattered against the floor. Neither of us moved to pick up the pieces.

"I think we should tell her to leave," I said.

Mama gazed into the empty fireplace, taking deep breaths

to control her anger. Then she unfolded Tiger Eye's crumpled dispatch and stared down at it as if the very words had been penned by the Devil himself.

Finally she said, "No, Reeves. Although this woman is certainly a wolf in sheep's clothing, we must best her at her own game. We will become such models of propriety that we outstrip Mrs. Brown's capacity for deception."

"What about Lucy?"

Mama paused. "We dare not tell her the truth. She's so young and untried. And I do believe Mrs. Brown's affections toward our Lucy are genuine. Do you not agree?"

I looked away. For I knew then and there that Tiger Eye Brown would find a way to use Lucy against us. As Daddy always said, "Never spare the truth, no matter how painful. For ignorance breeds deceit."

CHAPTER 11

Having little else than meat for my troops, and for nearly three weeks past having less than half rations of everything but beef, which has caused considerable diarrhea, my command of volunteers, badly disciplined and clothed, were unfit to march forward and drive in the enemy's advance.

—General Nathaniel Lyon, U.S. Army,
August 4, 1861

TIGER EYE DIDN'T GIVE any indication that her dispatch to *The Cincinnati Commercial* was missing. Instead, she and Lucy lingered at my writing desk the next morning, and I could hear Mrs. Brown's reading voice, grand and dramatic, all the way downstairs, even behind locked doors in Daddy's study.

There, I wrote another of my unposted letters to Daddy. I hadn't the heart to tell him the truth about Mrs. Brown, for if my letters ever reached him, wouldn't such news give him cause to worry?

Suddenly I heard the front door swing open and a pair of high-heeled boots click across Mama's walnut floors. Mama swept into the hall from the dining room. I was right behind her.

It was Captain Brown.

"Miranda!" he cried, pacing up and down, his fine uniform soiled with sweat and dirt, but no blood. "Miranda! Get down here, my darling." He had started upstairs when he saw Mama and me.

"This is a glorious time, Mrs. O'Neill. A glorious time."

"What is it, my beloved?" Tiger Eye cooed, slowly descending the stairs.

"A great victory at Dug Springs! General Price's Rebels turned and ran from us like the yellow-striped cowards they are."

Mama gasped and reached for my hand.

"What do you mean?" Mama asked.

"How many dead?" I whispered.

Captain Brown stood on tiptoe and pecked his wife on the cheek. Then he turned to Mama and me. "Fifty good Union men can whip fifteen hundred Rebs any day—with just one little cannon shot. Only cowards have flocked to the Secessionist cause, Madam."

"You must be mistaken, Captain." Mama dropped my hand, her eyes cold as steel. "There are brave fighting men on both sides."

"How many casualties?" I demanded.

"We killed a fair number," the captain bragged.

I ran upstairs, dodging past the captain, then Tiger Eye. I almost crashed right into Lucy, who stood at the top of the stairs, hair tied back with lilac ribbons like the ones on Tiger Eye's lace morning cap.

"Is Daddy all right, Reeves?" she whispered, her eyes wide with fear.

"What do you care?" I pulled a lilac ribbon from her curls. "You and Mrs. Brown." I knew that would make Lucy cry, but for some reason, it felt good.

Minutes later, I was dressed and racing for the horse barn. I shouted for Hector, but he didn't answer. So I ran to the far end of the barn and led out Ivanhoe.

Just as I reached for his bridle, Hector spoke over my shoulder, "No need for that, Miss Reeves. I've got the buggy ready for you out front."

I dropped the bridle and stared at him.

"Heard about the battle," he explained, "and figured you'd need a ride to the square." He helped me into the buggy and took the reins.

Jefferson Street was filled with Federal soldiers in sweat-darkened, dirty uniforms, all back from a long march. But from where? And how many of their enemy had they wounded or killed? It was useless to stop and ask. Most of the soldiers were German immigrants and couldn't speak much English.

Hector guided our buggy slowly, so slowly, through the throng of men, horses, wagons, and mules. Before we even reached the square, I heard Mr. Jenkins's pigs, squealing that horrible squeal pigs make just before they're butchered.

"Looks like these soldiers are fixing to have pork for lunch," Hector said, as we rounded the corner.

A detail of soldiers knelt in front of Coleman's Store and gutted the dead pigs. Their entrails steamed in the late morning heat, and the stench of meat and blood and guts turned my stomach.

Taking shallow breaths, I pointed to a rider cutting through the troops on a big gray stallion. "Over there, Hector." It was General Lyon himself, wearing a slouchy old duster and a sweat-stained hat. He slumped in the saddle, looking dried up and tired. We edged closer. Without thinking, I pulled out my notebook and started to write.

"Let us eat the last bit of mule flesh," one of General Lyon's officers was saying, his Irish voice heavy and deep, "and fire the last cartridge before we think of retreating."

General Lyon said nothing, glanced around at the faces of his officers, then pushed his horse through another group of soldiers who were butchering yet another of Mr. Jenkins's pigs.

"That's not a good idea, Miss O'Neill," a low voice rumbled gently. "Put the notebook away before someone mistakes you for a spy."

For a moment I froze, pencil poised over my notebook. My hand shook slightly. I knew the voice. It was Percival Wilder's.

He climbed into the buggy and took the reins from Hector.

"You shouldn't be here, you know. It isn't safe."

"My own home isn't safe anymore!" I fired back. "Why didn't you tell me about Tiger Eye Brown?"

He glanced at the wild, rowdy soldiers in the street around us. "A gentleman doesn't disclose a lady's secrets. Remember?" Then he added, "But maybe gentlemen—and ladies, for that matter—don't matter anymore." He nodded toward the

Germans, roasting a pig over a fire of broken-up furniture. "We had to requisition your fine neighbor's swine this morning, or no telling what all these hungry men might have done to your town."

"But I thought you'd won a great victory."

"Where did you hear such a lie?"

"From Captain Brown."

"He's a fool." Percival shook his head.

I tried to keep my voice steady. "Then casualties were light—on both sides?"

Percival looked straight into my eyes. His were dark and brown and deep. "If you're worried about your father, you have nothing to fear. A couple of Rebs may have succumbed to sunstroke while they ran from our cannon, but from what I've heard about your father, I doubt that he was one of them."

His arm brushed against mine, and that strange, fluttering sensation returned like a whole flock of butterflies.

Then it dawned on me. I was sitting beside Daddy's enemy, and without pretense of any kind, he had acknowledged Daddy's service with General Price. And I had as good as admitted it! Indeed, this was not the world of ladies and gentlemen that Mama had brought me up to.

Percival turned the buggy around toward home and saluted to the soldiers roasting Mr. Jenkins's pig.

"Got a sweetheart, Lieutenant?" a boy with a heavy German accent called out.

Percival raised his hat, and the soldiers cheered.

I stiffened and moved across the seat, wishing Hector were between us.

"Give them a little smile, Miss O'Neill. They'll be going into real battle all too soon." Percival's voice was sad, serious.

My butterflies vanished, but I couldn't smile. "Then the real battle is yet to come?"

We left the stench of butchered animals behind, but the smell of unwashed soldiers still rolled over us like the heat from a red-hot iron.

"I'd wager war, real war, will come before the week's out." Percival reined in the buggy and looked up Jefferson Street, past our house, out toward the ripening corn and the hazy blue sky. "Help me forget about war this afternoon, Miss Margaret Reeves," he whispered. "Just this once."

CHAPTER 12

Dear Lancelot,

I have encountered the most extraordinary young woman here. She is independent, headstrong, and beautiful—a writer of stories, a lover of poetry. I know you will believe I am besotted, but I am not. I only wish there were no war, so I could woo her properly.

—Percival Wilder to his brother,
August 4, 1861

THE HORSES TROTTED past our house, past lines of German soldiers, past mounted Federal patrols. Corn grew high on either side of the road, and the sky stretched white-hot overhead. In the distance, blackbirds trilled from the shade of swaying cedars down by Bessie Branch, the coldest, clearest spring in Greene County, and that's where we stopped.

Percival jumped out of the buggy. I started to climb out myself, but he was quicker. His hands went around my waist, and he lifted me down ever so slowly. We stood just a heartbeat apart, his hands still resting lightly on my waist, his face suddenly soft and serious. A warm, tingling feeling raced from my heart down through my arms and legs and back up again. I hated to admit it, but I liked standing that close to him. I liked the way he towered over me, so tall and straight and strong—and that scared me. I broke away and motioned for Hector to follow.

"Come have a drink!" I called, reaching for the dipper that hung on a peg by the tallest cedar. I rinsed the dipper, then lifted it to my lips. The water tasted cold and fresh.

Percival took the dipper from my hand and stared down at me so hard I was afraid he would kiss me—and he might have if Hector hadn't been along. Instead Percival drank deeply, then settled against a boulder on the far side of the branch.

"Are you fond of Keats?" he asked, taking a volume of poetry from his breast pocket.

Another warm flush swept over me. How often had Daddy and I sat at this very spring and read Mr. Keats or Mr. Shelley? Percival must have noticed my reaction, for he began:

> *"And can I ever bid these joys farewell?*
> *Yes, I must pass them for a nobler life,*
> *Where I may find the agonies, the strife—"*

"'Of human hearts,'" I whispered, finishing the line for him.

Together we read the afternoon away, and for the first time since Daddy had left, I felt bound to someone, someone who shared my love of books and poetry and words. When we stopped, the sound of katydids whirring in the dry, dusty trees overhead filled up the silence. I leaned back against a mossy trunk and watched as Percival slipped his book of poetry into his pocket.

He smiled at me as if we two were the only people in the whole wide world, as if Hector weren't stretched out in the shade of a nearby sycamore.

"Won't you please read something else, sir?" Hector asked. And for the first time, I realized that he, too, had shared this moment. His eyes were bright, lit up from within by the fires of words and images and beauty. Why had I never recognized this passion in him before?

But Percival again claimed all my attention. "Do you have something you'd like to read, Miss Margaret Reeves?" he asked, and his gaze fell to the pocket where I kept my notebook.

A soft, swirly feeling rose in my chest, and I felt myself blushing. But I reached for my notebook anyway.

"I've often wondered what secrets were recorded in that little brown book," he said, smiling.

"I don't intend to reveal any secrets, Mr. Percival Wilder."

His eyes twinkled with that devilish sparkle I'd once found so provoking. "Give me the notebook, and I'll read it myself!" His arm stole around my shoulders, his ungloved hand just inches from my notebook. I lingered just an instant there, enfolded in the pleasure of his arms, then pulled away, for I knew I should do my own reading.

"Don't be so impatient," I scolded, turning page after page of my notebook until I found the right one. I skimmed the first paragraph. My hands went all trembly, my mouth suddenly dry. Whatever made me think this was worthy of anyone's attention? But one glance at Percival Wilder told me my second thoughts had come too late. So I began.

"The soldiers surrounded the church, their uniforms a blight of darkness on a warm summer's day. . . ."

Did he notice the quiver in my voice? The way my hand shook when I turned each page? But I dared not look up. Every word, every sentence was dust in my mouth. *"All joy was crushed out,"* I continued, *"by the slow, steady drone of voices, voices forced to swear their loyalty. . . ."*

The words blurred together, and for a moment, I couldn't read my own writing. What *was* that word I'd scribbled in the margin just above the long line I'd crossed out? *Scrawny?* A *pale, scrawny child* . . . What had possessed me to use such a phrase? I rushed through the sentence, hoping Percival wouldn't have time to consider my poor choice of vocabulary. Finally, I came to the end, and there was a long, awful silence.

I shouldn't have read.

When I finally found the courage to look up, Percival was staring at me as if he were seeing me for the very first time. But it was Hector who broke the silence. "You've done your father proud, Miss Reeves," he said.

Hector's eyes burned into mine so fiercely that I had to look away. For the first time, we were speaking as equals, one person to another. And I knew in my heart, things would never be the same between us again.

"Hector's right," Percival said at last. "Your reading was inspired, Miss Margaret Reeves O'Neill. Every word rang true."

CHAPTER 13

*Three days ago, we learned of the great Rebel victory at
Bull Run. Now we wait for battle here. Percival
Wilder says his troops hope to vindicate the Union's terrible losses in Virginia. And General Lyon is reported to
have said that he will see every man, woman, and child
in our state dead and buried before conceding Missouri
to the government of Jefferson Davis. Are the lives of all
of us worth so little?*

—Writer's Notebook, Margaret Reeves O'Neill,
August 8, 1861

THE PHOTOGRAPHS of Mama and Lucy were so beautiful they
made my heart stand still. In the miniature *carte-de-visite,*
Lucy and Mama stood side by side, Mama's arm resting
against a pillar draped with a Missouri flag, her hand on
Lucy's shoulder. They gazed into the camera with such longing and intensity that I knew Daddy would indeed carry that
image right next to his heart and into the heat of battle. It
made me wish that I'd been photographed, too.

"There's no time to spare, Miz Reeves," Juneau said.
"Make up your mind. They're waiting in the carriage right
now."

Of course, that was so. Mama and Lucy were packed and ready to meet Mrs. Campbell, who had promised to try to smuggle their photograph across Federal lines. But Mama had decided to let me choose which photograph to send.

"The *carte-de-visite*," I said at last, handing the photograph to Juneau. "That's the one Daddy should have."

Juneau nodded and started for the study door. Then she turned. "Why don't you send all those letters you've been writin' along with this picture? Don't know but what that wouldn't please Mista Gaylen more." Before I could thank her, she'd disappeared into the front hall.

Quickly, I took the letters from Daddy's portable writing case and reached into my pocket for a length of purple ribbon to tie them into a neat bundle. The ribbon caught on my notebook, which slipped out of my pocket along with a lead pencil and a pair of scissors. My fingers were all thumbs, and the ribbon was slippery. It took five attempts before that ribbon would knot, two before the study door would lock shut.

Then I tore down the hall as fast as my hoops would allow. But to no avail. Mama and Lucy had already gone.

I RETURNED Daddy's letters to his writing case, gathered up the photographs Mama and Lucy had left behind, and, locking the study door once more, carried the remaining portraits out to the front porch. If I stared intently at those pictures, then surely I wouldn't cry. After all, I told myself,

Daddy would know I loved him, even if he didn't carry a remembrance of me into battle. Still, I felt empty inside, and sad.

Then I heard the sound of gravel scrunching on the driveway. It was Mrs. Campbell.

"Is that Brown woman about?" she asked, not waiting for her man Elmo to help her out of the buggy.

I shook my head.

"Good. I wouldn't trust that woman as far as I could throw her. Now, where are those things your Mama wants me to take to your daddy?"

"Why, she's delivering them to you this very minute."

Mrs. Campbell frowned and tipped back her bonnet. "Well, this is a fine state of affairs. I could have sworn we agreed to meet here at eleven o'clock. Well, I haven't time to wait."

She turned toward the carriage, but I called her back. "If you'll just wait a moment more," I pleaded, "I'll gather a few things for Daddy myself."

"Make it fast then, Margaret Reeves," she said, nodding.

I raced back into the house, down the hall, to Daddy's study door. I tossed aside Mama and Lucy's photographs and fumbled with the lock. Why, why, *why* did simple tasks always require twice as much time when you were in a hurry? Finally the door swung open. My letters would find their way to Daddy after all! Then a thought so bold and daring took hold of me that I couldn't let it go. What if I sent Daddy more than letters? What if I went myself?

I paced back and forth across the study, quickly framing all the arguments I'd use to convince Mrs. Campbell to take me along. Suddenly there were angry voices in the hall, the sound of high heels tapping across the floor. Then Tiger Eye Brown swept into Daddy's study, and Mrs. Campbell was right behind her.

"My, what a marvelous room!" Tiger Eye ran her fingers across the titles on Daddy's bookshelves. "It's a shame you keep it under lock and key."

"I must ask you to leave this room, Mrs. Brown," I said, hoping to sound cool and poised and firm. "This is a very private part of our household, and since I'm engaged for the afternoon with Mrs. Campbell, I can't possibly allow you to stay here unattended."

Mrs. Campbell raised her eyebrows and quickly looked out the window.

"Oh. You two are going somewhere?" The smile behind Mrs. Brown's colorless eyes reminded me of January sunshine—bright and sparkling without any warmth. "Where are you going on such a hot and miserable afternoon?"

"To the Campbell farm south of town," I lied. "That's where we get that white corn Lucy likes so well." Mrs. Campbell almost smiled, and I could tell the fib I'd borrowed from Hector had impressed her. I was getting into the habit of lying these days. I knew Daddy wouldn't approve, but what else could I do?

"How noble of you to brave the noontime heat for your little sister." Tiger Eye strolled slowly around Daddy's settee, then gathered up her skirts and sank into its deep leather cushions. "But are you sure, Mrs. Campbell, that Federal troops will let you pass? After all, one does hear the most scandalous accounts of your Rebel sympathies."

"If you refer to the stories that I am a spy, Mrs. Brown, I am sorry to disappoint you. But upon my soul, I wish they all were true." Then Mrs. Campbell's eyes narrowed and her skirts swished softly as she moved closer to the settee. "But I, too, have heard stories, Mrs. Brown. Stories about a certain newspaper correspondent called Tiger Eye, who uses dishonest methods to glean half-truths from families struggling under the adversities of war."

Tiger Eye turned away and reached for Volume 1 of *Adam Bede.* For a long, long time she was silent. When she finally turned, she smiled at me faintly. "George Eliot," she murmured. "Never heard of him. Nor Tiger Eye, for that matter."

I snatched the book away and slipped it into Daddy's writing case. "I must ask you again to leave, Mrs. Brown. We are in a hurry."

"Do go on, then." Tiger Eye stood up and leaned across the desk. "I'll simply stay here and browse. Or are there things here that you don't want me to see? Dark family secrets tucked away, perhaps, in that cunning little writing case?"

I secured the latch on the case and held it tightly under my arm. "It is time for you to go," I said.

For a long moment, Tiger Eye stared right at me, and I stared back without a flinch. She gave me another January smile. "Then I shall withdraw, Margaret Reeves," she said, "for your convenience."

Mrs. Campbell led Tiger Eye into the hall, toward the stairs. Fumbling with the lock, I heard Mrs. Campbell say, "Dine with me tomorrow. You and Captain Brown."

There was a long pause. I tucked the key back inside my blouse and waited for Tiger Eye's reply.

Mrs. Campbell spoke again. "I promise to have the most newsworthy guests in all of Springfield at my table."

Mrs. Brown positively growled. "I accept your invitation, but I assure you, your preoccupation with the news is ill advised."

I waited in the doorway until I could hear Tiger Eye's footsteps upstairs, then raced toward Mrs. Campbell's buggy.

"Let's go, Elmo," she ordered. "You're pretty cool under fire. I'll say that for you, Margaret Reeves."

We set off at a brisk pace and were well away from town before I realized I'd left Mama and Lucy's photographs behind.

FEDERAL SENTRIES were posted just past Mrs. Campbell's brother-in-law's farm, down south of town toward Wilson's Creek. Her brother-in-law, Mr. Junius Campbell, was a strong Union man, the only one in the family. But still, family always came first—at least among the Campbells and their kin. I suspected that Mrs. Campbell had persuaded Mr. Campbell to find Federal sentries who would look the other way—if the price was right. Elmo reined in the buggy. I felt jittery inside, and scared, but the two soldiers who stopped us didn't look to be much older than I was.

"One of the Parker babies just down the road has the croup and needs my special elixir," Mrs. Campbell said, as cool as a cucumber.

"Niver heared of no Parker family. How 'bout you, Buck?" The soldier's eyes narrowed.

The other sentry spit and shook his head. "Me neither."

"They live about four miles south of here, sir," I heard myself saying, hoping against hope that the sentry called Buck, who stood ever so close to the carriage, couldn't hear the wild thumping of my heart.

"Do they now, missy?" Buck smiled a slow, sly smile. "You always go calling on sick babies, do you? Why, you're nothin' but a baby your own self."

Mrs. Campbell turned and reached for one of the big hampers she'd brought along. Buck and his companion edged even closer. Elmo tightened his grip on the whip. Then Mrs. Campbell righted herself. "This young lady is my apprentice," she fibbed and held out a big basket of cold ham, candied yams, and blackberry wine.

Buck smiled and took the basket. "You tell that Miz Parker that we're shore sorry her youngun's took sick, but we appreciate the doctor's remedies." He grinned and passed the other private the bottle of wine.

As Elmo pulled away from the sentries, I tried not to stare

too much at Mrs. Campbell. How capably she'd handled those two privates.

"The whole Federal army's half starved," Mrs. Campbell confided, as if to explain her strategy. "Though I understand supplies are due in today from Rolla. Our men should have struck earlier. An enemy with an empty stomach is not nearly as fearsome as one that's well fed." She glanced back at the soldiers. "Drive slowly, Elmo. We don't want to appear too conspicuous."

We topped a rise in the road, and where stands of oak and maple and limestone bluffs gave way to open ground, there was General Price's army, camped all along Wilson's Creek. Hundreds of men, hundreds of tents, hundreds of mules and horses. Yet we weren't more than ten miles from home.

"I had no idea Daddy was so close by," I whispered.

"They're half starved, too. And poorly clothed."

I ran my hand across Daddy's writing case.

"I should have brought something other than this." I felt suddenly foolish. What did my letters, or *Adam Bede*, or even forgotten photographs mean now on the eve of battle? Daddy needed food, clothing, maybe even ammunition.

"Don't worry, Reeves." Mrs. Campbell smiled. "You had other things on your mind this afternoon. I declare, that Tiger Eye Brown is a scourge sent from the Devil himself." She patted my hand. "Besides, I brought an extra hamper along just in case."

We drove down one more long, dusty hill. Another pair of sentries stopped us, two of the Cooper boys from home who were serving with General Price. Their sister had been at the Fayetteville Ladies' Institute with me the year before. They whooped and hollered and hugged us. Mrs. Campbell gave them each a piece of fried chicken and briefly told them the news. Then they escorted us into camp. Men raised their caps to us as we drove by. But they looked hot and sickly, their uniforms—if you could call them that—just thrown together in various colors of blue, gray, and homespun brown.

I squinted and looked around for Daddy, but there were just too many soldiers. They sat in groups, a few molding bullets, others playing cards. They all seemed so scraggly and unruly, less disciplined than the hundreds of German troops in the Federal army. I wondered, *How many of these men will be alive two days from now? Or next week? Or next year?* Daddy's words came back to me then. "We'll see how the people of Missouri really feel about this war—after glory steals life from both sides." Instinctively I reached for my notebook, but Mrs. Campbell stopped me.

"Imagine what damage Mrs. Brown could do if she got her hands on your observations, Reeves. Store it all up in your memory and write it out later, when all danger of discovery is past."

At last Elmo reined in the horses, and we stopped in front of a group of canvas tents. A young aide-de-camp saluted Mrs. Campbell and the Cooper brothers.

"Tell the General two loyal ladies of Missouri have arrived with news from Springfield," Mrs. Campbell said.

The aide nodded, and another one helped Mrs. Campbell and me from the buggy. A big, handsome man with wavy gray hair approached Mrs. Campbell. He took her hand and smiled.

"I should have known that if anyone could break the Federal blockade, it would be Mrs. Louisa Campbell."

She curtsied and smiled back. "It's good to see you again, General Price. I hope all my sons are serving you proudly." They started to walk toward the general's tent when Mrs. Campbell stopped and turned.

"I've brought Gaylen O'Neill's daughter with me. I'm sure she very much wants to see her daddy."

"I believe Colonel O'Neill is camped just over the next hill." General Price smiled down at me and motioned for one of his aides. "Lieutenant, will you assist Miss O'Neill in her search?"

Slowly, the lieutenant and I threaded our way through dozens and dozens of campsites, down one hill and up the next. How could the general keep track of so many officers and men? Just when I was beginning to despair of ever finding Daddy, a familiar voice called out my name.

"Miz Reeves! Miz Reeves! Over here!"

I ran toward Hiram's voice, and a pair of big, strong arms—Daddy's arms—enfolded me in a tight embrace.

"NO GIFTS could please me more," Daddy said, setting *Adam Bede* aside and holding my bundle of letters in his hand. His face was gaunt and sunburned. I handed him another piece of Mrs. Campbell's chicken.

"I'm glad to see you're writing, Reeves," Daddy continued. "Someday, when all of this is over . . ." He looked out at General Price's encampment, at acres and acres of army. He sighed and touched my cheek. "Perhaps voices like yours will find some meaning in it."

"But you'll be home soon," I returned hopefully.

Daddy didn't answer, and I felt a horrible silence between us, a gulf of experience I couldn't cross. Then he suddenly launched into a funny and colorful account of life in General Price's army and of Hiram's valiant attempts to maintain Daddy's rank as an officer and gentleman. He held up a fine crystal goblet, one Hiram had packed from home.

"It's the only piece of equipment in this whole army that isn't broken." Daddy laughed. "But now, you tell me the news from home."

So I told him things that weren't in my letters—sunny, bright stories that strained the truth but would give Daddy's heart some ease. Then I looked away, and Daddy touched my arm.

"Thank you for your stories, Reeves. But I expect to find more depth of feeling here, in this pack of letters."

I gazed into his eyes and knew that we'd both been telling tales all afternoon. Sometimes it hurts too much to say what you really feel.

Mrs. Campbell called to me from General Price's tent, and I slowly got to my feet. I hugged Hiram good-bye first, then

Daddy. He held me tight and hard and close. For once, words failed me, and I choked back tears. Then he kissed me on the forehead, and together we walked toward Mrs. Campbell's buggy. As we drove away, Daddy was untying the purple ribbon that bound my letters.

CHAPTER 14

When generals gather to talk of war,
The land is filled with the cannon's roar.
But the spirits of loyal patriots soar,
And a nation hovers on victory's door.
> —From "When Patriots Dare"
> by Mrs. Horatio Brown,
> August 9, 1861

THE NEXT DAY, I spent the whole morning locked upstairs with Mama and Juneau in Mama's sewing closet. The room was tiny and close, choked with the mingled smells of Mama's lavender and Juneau's verbena sachet.

"You'll need so many things this year, Reeves," Mama said, her eyes shining. "A young lady always does during her final year of finishing school. It's almost like planning a trousseau."

Juneau raised her eyebrows, but Mama didn't notice.

"It was during my last year at Mrs. Gaston's academy that I first met your daddy, and I'm convinced that if it hadn't been for my aquamarine silk, he'd never have noticed me at the Bright House Ball that September." She pulled out the pattern box and sorted through the ones she thought were suitable. "What do you think, Reeves?"

I tried to concentrate, I really did. But my mind was filled with images of soldiers fitting new flints to their old muskets, roasting green corn for their dinners, drilling barefoot at Wilson's Creek . . .

"Reeves, you're not paying attention." Mama ran her hand over the bolts of fabric Juneau held across her arms. "Now, I think the brown check will work up fine for a new day dress; and for your new traveling costume, what do you think of this sapphire blue merino?"

I nodded and moved to the window. A company of infantrymen paced through their drills on the street below, sending up great clouds of dust. Mrs. Campbell believed that General Price should attack Springfield right away, before the Federal soldiers retreated north. That's what she'd told the general yesterday—and she'd told Mama, too.

"You'd better send the girls out to one of your farms right away, Vashti." Mrs. Campbell's voice had been stern, urgent. "Springfield won't be safe for any of us this whole week."

Mama touched my shoulder. "Reeves, come away from that window. I want to discuss your new ball gown." But she stayed by the window with me to watch the Federal soldiers.

When I glanced up at her, there were tears in her eyes. "I wish I'd had the chance to go with you yesterday," she said softly. "I'd have given your daddy this."

She took the *carte-de-visite* from her apron pocket and stared down at it as if it were a gem beyond price.

"I meant to take your photographs along," I said, fighting back my own tears. "Honestly, I did."

"Do not reproach yourself, Margaret Reeves," Mama said, turning from the window. Then she took the bolt of sapphire blue merino from Juneau's arms and spread it out for cutting.

LUCY SWOOPED through the hall in her best sprigged muslin, then dived into Mama's bedroom.

"Mama! Mama! Mrs. Brown has invited me to ride to Mrs. Campbell's with her. May I go? Please?"

"All right, Lucy. But turn around. Let me look at that sash one more time."

"Don't worry about it, Mrs. O'Neill. I've already tied it for her." Mrs. Brown floated into Mama's bedroom wearing a pale gown of gold silk edged with bands of lace frills and pink rosettes. Her soft, rounded shoulders were completely bare.

"How festive you look, Mrs. Brown." But I could tell Mama didn't approve. The dress was far too daring for dinner at the Campbells'.

"Isn't it pretty, Mama?" Lucy fingered Mrs. Brown's silk flounces. "I want one just like it for my first year at Fayetteville."

Mama smiled. "In time, Lucy. In time."

"You should consider sending her this year instead of next, Mrs. O'Neill." Tiger Eye tilted her head and smiled. "After all, I understand Reeves spent her first year at the Fayetteville Ladies' Institute when she was just Lucy's age."

Her eyes narrowed. "And in times of war, children grow up so fast."

Lucy's eyes lit up like a pair of harvest moons. "Can I, Mama? Please?"

Mama shook her head. "I appreciate your interest in my children, Mrs. Brown." Every word was icy cold. "But I've chosen to keep Lucy here with me until next fall. She hasn't had the advantage of her daddy's tutoring this year. He was distracted by all the talk of war."

"How unfortunate for all of you." Tiger Eye's voice rang as true as an untuned piano. "Come, little Lucy," she said. "We don't want to leave my gallant husband waiting."

Lucy ran to Mama for a good-bye kiss. "Please let me go to the institute." Her whisper carried across the room. Then she left hand in hand with Mrs. Brown.

"That woman is a misery, Miz Vashti." Juneau pulled the Spanish lace at my throat so tight I almost choked. "If she stays through the fall, I'd send Miz Lucy to Fayetteville. Mizzus Brown is like a bad apple waitin' to spoil all the good ones left in the barrel."

I waited for Mama to chastise Juneau, as she always did when Juneau presumed to know what was best for us. But Mama was quiet for a long, long time. So quiet, I wondered if she'd even heard Juneau's remark.

Mama fluffed up the sleeves of my watered silk and adjusted the ribbons in my hair. Finally she said, "You may be right, Juneau."

*   *   *

WE GOT TO Mrs. Campbell's late, as we did for any social occasion. It was Mama's nature to make an entrance, even for dinner with an old friend.

"Vashti, at last." Mrs. Campbell broke away from a group of guests and drew Mama and me into a circle of Federal uniforms. "I believe the two of you already know most of my guests."

Percival Wilder, standing alongside Mrs. Phelps, smiled down at us and took Mama's hand. But his eyes told me he'd rather have taken mine, though Mama would never have allowed it. Still, he stood right next to me, the long line of his blue trousers brushing against my watered silk.

We'd apparently interrupted a discussion of Mrs. Stowe's *Uncle Tom's Cabin*, and Tiger Eye hadn't bothered to stop talking when we arrived. She just nodded in our general direction.

"Yes, it is a marvelous book, and every page rings true." Tiger Eye flipped open her Japanese fan and smiled over its gilt edges. "Its pages were so gripping that it inspired me to cross an ocean to fight against the injustices of such a barbaric system."

She fanned away at the little beads of sweat gathered on her forehead and smiled at Mama, Mrs. Campbell, and Mrs. Phelps. She knew we all depended on slavery for a livelihood. "But then, I'm sure you don't consider yourself barbaric, do you?"

I wondered why Mrs. Campbell didn't call us all in to dinner and break off this uncomfortable conversation. Finally I said, "*Uncle Tom's Cabin* is certainly a memorable book, but I

thought its characters were more sentimental than realistic."
How often Daddy had warned me of too much sentiment in
my own writing.

Percival smiled in my direction, and goose bumps prick-
led up and down my arms. "But the book's power comes
from emotion, not realism, Miss O'Neill. The human heart
is governed by feelings, not facts."

I probably blushed forty shades of scarlet, but nobody
seemed to notice, not even Mama—because at that very
moment, Mrs. Campbell's final dinner guest arrived, and I
understood why she'd held dinner so long. It was General
Lyon himself, looking worn and haggard and hot in his dusty
Federal uniform. I wondered if I should shake his hand, but
Mama did, and after all, he was Mrs. Campbell's guest. He
took my hand and I looked into his pale blue eyes. There was
something about them that made me think of a high-strung
Thoroughbred trapped in a burning barn. I shivered, despite
the heat and the Spanish lace wrapped tight around my neck.

Because there were so many of us, Mrs. Campbell had set
up dinner in the backyard under two spreading sycamores.
Percival took my arm and led me outside, then sat down
right beside me. I could tell Mama didn't approve, but she
was too busy rounding up Lucy and Mrs. Campbell's Little
Lou to do much about it.

Maybe because General Lyon was with us, no one talked
about the war. The conversation drifted from how hot the
weather was to how brisk business seemed to be at the
new photography studio downtown. I couldn't eat a bite,

not with Percival Wilder sitting right at my elbow. That strange, fluttery feeling around my heart just wouldn't go away.

Then, just as Mrs. Campbell's people were serving dessert, General Lyon abruptly changed the topic of conversation. "Madam, you wish us success?" he asked, looking straight at Mrs. Campbell.

I glanced at Mama, who had suddenly gone pale. So had Mrs. Phelps.

"Sir," Mrs. Campbell said clearly, "I am a Southern woman."

General Lyon laid his napkin aside. "And you have sons in the Confederacy?"

There was a long pause. Everyone watched Mrs. Campbell. It would be treason if Mrs. Campbell openly spoke the truth.

She put her hands in her lap and looked straight into General Lyon's eyes. Her voice was clear and firm. "I have four sons who serve the Confederacy, and I wish they were fifty— and that I were leading them."

Captain Brown's fork splashed into his glass of lemonade, but no one else moved. Finally, General Lyon said, "I hope no trouble is at hand for so brave a woman." Then he rose and signaled to the officers to leave.

Everyone suddenly got to their feet, except me. I hadn't expected such gallantry from the general. I watched as he actually kissed Mrs. Campbell's hand and saluted. He even nodded good-bye to Mama as he left on Mrs. Phelps's arm.

Tiger Eye was right behind them, hurrying out to the street, I guessed so that she could rush down to the telegraph office and file a story about what had just happened.

Then Percival Wilder pulled me to my feet, and his lips brushed softly against mine. "I'm bold to steal this kiss," he whispered, "because tomorrow there will be war."

He strode into the house so fast I didn't even have time to get the jitters I'd always expected with a first kiss.

CHAPTER 15

*General Lyon . . . attacked the enemy at 6:30 o'clock on
the morning of the 10th, nine miles . . . {from} Springfield. Engagement severe.*
— Major General John C. Frémont, U.S. Army,
August 13, 1861

A SOUND LIKE distant thunder woke me up early. But it
wasn't thunder and it wasn't artillery practice, because that
low rumble was almost continuous, as if the earth itself were
shaking in its boots. I crept downstairs, out to the front
porch, and gazed off toward the southwest, down toward
Wilson's Creek. Beyond the trees and the town and the hills,
in the gray light of dawn, Daddy was there—*there* where that
dull, awful thud sounded again and again. Tears welled up in
my eyes and rolled down my cheeks. I couldn't have stopped
them any more than I could have stopped the war. I took my
notebook from the pocket of my dressing gown, but I
couldn't write. I couldn't find the words.

"What a moving tableau," Tiger Eye Brown whispered in
my ear. "Those in bondage waiting for their liberation."

At first I thought she was talking about me, but then I
realized what she meant. Our servants were out front—all

of them—gazing off into the distance. Even Juneau and Hector stood way out by the road. Watching. Listening. Waiting.

For a long moment the guns were silent, and the robins sang their sweet, early morning song. But the steady boom began again, and the porch shook beneath my feet.

Finally Juneau turned, her face as smooth as stone. She stared at Tiger Eye and me for what seemed like forever, then she shooed the rest of our people back to their chores. Only Hector remained out by the edge of the road. Juneau called to him, her voice so low and tender I couldn't catch the words. He came to her slowly, and for the first time I saw Juneau hold him close and tight, as if she feared he'd slip through her arms like water.

Tiger Eye touched my arm, and her lips twisted up in what passed for a smile. "Now tell me a secret, Miss Margaret Reeves," she whispered, her eyes glinting steel. "For whom were you crying just a moment ago? Yourself, or your father, or Percival Wilder, who stole a kiss from your maiden lips just yesterday?"

I clenched my fists behind my back. "Whatever do you mean?"

"I came back for my gloves." Her smile was chilling. "And saw the two of you alone under the boughs of a sycamore. It was almost as moving as the tableau we've just witnessed. Perhaps I should write a poem about it."

"Do you weep for no one, Mrs. Brown?" I asked. "Not even your husband?"

A low, deep rumble from the battlefield hit the house like a wave and rattled all our windows. Tiger Eye stepped off the porch and slipped one hand into a fawn-colored glove. "In times like these, one must put away personal regard and live only for one's professional principals. It is a lesson you would do well to emulate."

She walked down the drive toward Juneau, and I wondered what principles Tiger Eye had ever lived for—other than advancing her own cause. If all writers abided by such "principles," then I wanted no part of them.

"I need coffee, Juneau, and sandwiches," she called. Her skirt was drawn up short over her hoops, just skimming the tops of her boots. She looked off toward the low thunder of cannon fire, then turned toward the barn. "Have that boy of yours saddle me a horse."

A few minutes later Mama and Lucy joined me on the front porch, and we watched Tiger Eye ride off toward the sound of booming cannons.

IN SILENCE, we took our coffee out on the porch. The cannons continued to thunder steadily. Mama rocked back and forth in her rocking chair, her hands idle, her eyes closed. Lucy, her face as pale as a green peach, sat crumpled at Mama's feet. I watched Hector, who'd returned to his post by the road. Juneau couldn't take her eyes off him.

Along about seven-thirty that morning, Mrs. Campbell and Elmo drove up the driveway. She waved Hector away when he offered to help her out. "Haven't got the time. I'm headed down toward Junius's farm."

"But that's got to be almost in the thick of . . ." My voice trailed off as Mrs. Campbell's face tightened.

"I know, Reeves. But I sent Little Lou down there last night. I thought she'd be safer away from town."

Lucy gasped, and Mama took her hand.

Mrs. Campbell's voice almost broke. "I'd been told that General Price was going to march on Springfield last night and that Little Lou would be safer away from home. But this time, my information was wrong. Dead wrong."

She paused and we all listened to the awful sound of cannons.

"My boys are out there," Mrs. Campbell said slowly, "as they should be. But Little Lou . . ."

Mama walked across the porch to the buggy. "Don't you worry, Louisa. Little Lou will be just fine. Both sides will take precautions to spare the innocent." She paused. "But if you like, I'll send Hector along with you and Elmo. You might need an extra hand."

Hector's eyes lit up like the Fourth of July; Juneau's went dark.

"I'd be happy to go, too," I volunteered quickly, trying hard to think of a reason why Mrs. Campbell might need me. The only one that came to mind was that I could help tend the wounded . . . or the dying. And none of us wanted to say such words aloud, though we all were thinking them.

Mama shook her head. "There's no reason for you to go, Reeves." Then she exchanged a long look with Juneau.

Finally Mama said, "Take one of the mules, Hector. You don't want that pretty little filly of yours requisitioned right out from under you."

He nodded but glared back at Mama from under the brim of his hat. It was enough to make me believe that if he'd ridden to the battlefield on Titania, he'd never have come back to us.

SHORTLY AFTER nine o'clock, the cannons stopped. Their silence was far more terrifying than their rumble. We waited and waited and waited, but the guns remained quiet. Finally I jumped to my feet.

"Let me go to the square, Mama, and find out what's happened."

Mama nodded slowly. "Take Juneau with you."

Juneau took off her apron and folded it over the back of a chair. I jumped off the porch and started toward the street.

"Margaret Reeves," Mama called. "A lady is never seen in public without her hat."

I dashed back inside, grabbed my hat, and squashed it on my head. By the time I reached the porch again, the sound of cannon fire was rolling over us like a sudden spring storm.

We sat on our porch for another three hours.

Finally, just about lunchtime, the cannons stopped, this time for good. Mama wouldn't let me leave her side. She had Juneau bring out her knitting, and we all sat making socks for General Price's army. I thought it might be better to make bandages but quickly pushed away that thought.

Then I wondered how many soldiers would even need socks now. . . .

It was the longest, hottest afternoon of my whole life.

The clock had just chimed five o'clock when Hector and his mule galloped up the driveway.

"General Lyon's shot dead!" he yelled.

I met him on the steps, and he whispered, "Dead men everywhere." He looked straight into my eyes, and I knew he'd seen things too unspeakable for words.

Mama, still clutching her knitting in one hand, grabbed his arm. "Who won?"

"Hard to say, Miss Vashti. So many dead. But the Federal soldiers are pulling back."

"And Little Lou?" Lucy rasped. "Did you see Little Lou?"

"Oh, she's fine, Miss Lucy. Watched the whole battle atop a haystack at Mr. Junius's farm." He glanced up at his mother. "Mrs. Campbell told me that there's a hospital set up in her house, and she needs everybody there right now."

Mama dropped her knitting and whisked into the house. "Come on, Juneau. Pack up that cold ham and fetch my medical bag. Reeves, Lucy—there's not a moment to spare."

Juneau lightly touched Hector's face, her hand atremble, her eyes almost soft. "Did you see any Jayhawkers, son?" she asked.

He shook his head.

"Good."

CHAPTER 16

My Dearest Husband,
 The Federal army is in retreat, our general dead. But so many others are gone as well, dear friends we will see no more. Many a good man has lost his life today, on both sides.

—Mrs. John Phelps to her husband,
August 10, 1861

I'D JUST TURNED to go inside when the sound of wagon wheels drew me back to the porch. It was Mrs. Phelps and her man George.

"Louisa Campbell needs you all right away," she called.

"Yes, we heard," I said, running toward the wagon. Mrs. Phelps's face was flushed. "Where are you going?" I asked.

George drew in the reins, and Mrs. Phelps paused. "You've heard that General Lyon has been slain?"

I nodded.

"George and I are on the way to the battlefield to retrieve his body," Mrs. Phelps continued. "I fear what might happen if his remains fall into Rebel hands."

I didn't even think. "I'm going with you." I jumped into the wagon.

Mrs. Phelps took my hand. "I can't take you there, Reeves. It's no place for a young lady."

"You listen to her, Miz Reeves," George said, nodding.

My eyes filled with tears. "Go, George. Go now." I grabbed the reins, but his strong arms stopped me.

"Please." I turned to Mrs. Phelps. "I have to know. About Daddy and—" I stopped, unable to say Percival's name out loud. "And all the others."

Mrs. Phelps looked straight into my eyes. At last she spoke. "All right, Reeves. You have the pluck to see what war is really like. Let's go, George."

BY THE TIME we got to the square, I'd had my first taste of real war. A butcher's wagon, filled with wounded Federal soldiers, turned off toward Mrs. Campbell's. It was crammed full of men, some sitting up and clutching an arm or leg, others lying still and quiet. A few were bandaged; most were awash with blood. I wanted to turn away but couldn't. I watched until the wagon was completely out of sight.

The square was wild with activity, and George had a hard time getting across. Everywhere, people were loading wagons with supplies, guns, and even furniture. A long line snaked around the telegraph office, where I glimpsed Tiger Eye's short, plaid skirt.

"Miz Phelps, what's happenin'?" George pulled the horses up.

"The Union families are moving north. They're afraid of

your General Price, Reeves." She patted my hand. "But I won't leave. This is my home, no matter which army camps on the doorstep."

Another wagon of wounded rumbled by, and this time there were screams and moans and curses.

We headed out toward Telegraph Road, but our progress was hampered by groups of Federal soldiers, all heading toward Springfield, all moving as fast as their wounded would let them. Their uniforms were soaked with sweat, caked with dust and blood.

"There!" Mrs. Phelps pointed.

George stopped the wagon near a detachment of Federal officers whose uniforms looked clean and fresh. They obviously hadn't seen any fighting all day. I looked around, hoping to see Percival Wilder.

"Mrs. Phelps," said a tall lieutenant. "Our orders are to escort you under a flag of truce back to the battlefield for General Lyon's body. Dr. Melcher is waiting with the corpse at the Ray house."

"Please proceed, Lieutenant."

We lurched ahead. Those Federal troops in their unsoiled uniforms gave me hope. Maybe daddy's unit, like these men, hadn't seen any action at all.

"Don't worry, miss," said the lieutenant, tipping his hat to me. "We don't expect any violence from the Rebs this afternoon. They're as busy burying their dead as we are."

* * *

WE WERE perhaps three or four miles out of town when I
saw my first dead soldiers. Their bodies were heaped in a
wagon under a bloody canvas.

"Look away, Miz Reeves," George whispered.

But I couldn't. Everywhere there were mangled arms and
legs, eyes glazed open. The smell of death, as foul as it was
sweet, hovered over the wagon like a demon cloud. But the
worst was a leering face, unnaturally black and shiny against
that bloody canvas. I gasped.

"Happens in the heat," a soldier behind me whispered.
"They lie there dead in the sun and their faces turn blacker
than a darky's."

My stomach churned up like a whirlwind, but I wouldn't
vomit. Not there, in front of soldiers who hadn't even faced a
bullet. Mrs. Phelps took my hand and we drove on, past
more and more troops, more and more wounded, more and
more corpses piled in wagons. Daddy had spent a whole day
in this nightmare. So had Percival Wilder.

Up ahead, a detachment of Rebel soldiers moved toward
us from Wilson's Creek. They carried a white flag; a wagon
brought up the rear. As they got closer, I recognized General
Price and scanned the faces of his aides, looking for Daddy.

"He's not here." My voice shook.

"Don't despair, Reeves," Mrs. Phelps whispered. "Surely
the general will know your daddy's fate."

General Price saluted, then stiffly dismounted. He moved
slowly, painfully, his linen duster heavily stained with blood
on one side.

"You've been wounded, General," said Mrs. Phelps.

"As many a good man has today, Mrs. Phelps." He tipped his big black hat. "I deliver one of the less fortunate this afternoon."

Several men lifted a body wrapped in a blood-stained counterpane. "I bring you the body of General Lyon." General Price took off his hat. "Even in death, a worthy adversary deserves our respect, Madam."

"Thank you, General."

General Price's men gently laid the body in the back of our wagon, then they all saluted. The smell of death became overwhelming. I took short, shallow breaths and tried not to gag.

General Price turned to go.

"General," I whispered. "Perhaps you don't remember me, but we met two days ago at Wilson's Creek in the company of Mrs. Campbell."

Mrs. Phelps gasped, as the general turned to meet my gaze. "My apologies for not recognizing you, young lady."

"Have you any news of my father, Colonel Gaylen O'Neill?"

The General took my hand, and for an instant, I felt a flicker of hope. After all, he had directed me to Daddy once before. But the general was shaking his head. "In the confusion of a battle such as this, it is not unusual for an officer to be missing in action. Please, do not be unduly alarmed, Miss O'Neill. Your father is a fine and able soldier."

"Thank you, sir," I choked.

George turned the horses around, and Mrs. Phelps sprinkled a few drops of cologne on a handkerchief. "Cover your nose and mouth with this, Reeves. It will cut the stench."

IT WAS TWILIGHT when we got back into town. We drove straight to the Phelpses' town property on College Avenue, where Mrs. Worell and Mrs. Sheppard were waiting out back. George and two other servants carried the body into the back parlor and laid it on a long, low table. A walnut casket stretched across the floor in front of the fireplace.

"I'll walk Reeves over to Louisa's," said Mrs. Phelps.

The Campbell house was all lit up, surrounded by wagons and carts and buggies. Wounded, dying, and dead men lay out on the lawn, their uniforms all dull and colorless in the growing darkness. It didn't matter whether they wore blue or gray.

"Wait here, Reeves." Mrs. Phelps stopped at the gate. "Let me find your mama or Juneau. You've seen enough death for one day."

She threaded her way toward the porch, then stopped short. She knelt by a body stretched out under one of Mrs. Campbell's sycamores, and I could tell by the way she leaned over it and touched it ever so gently that it was someone she knew, someone I might know.

I slowly opened the gate and walked up toward the porch, my pulse pounding at my temples. As I got closer, I saw the body's uniform. It was Federal blue.

"Go back, Reeves," said Mrs. Phelps softly. "You don't want to see this."

But I had to. I pushed by her and knelt beside the body. His eyes were wide open, a single bullet hole through his forehead. Yet I felt inexpressible relief, for the dead soldier was not Percival Wilder.

"This boy once served my husband," Mrs. Phelps murmured, tears glistening in her eyes. "I must write his mama."

Just then I heard a high, keening sound. It floated out of the house, wild and sad and painful. I looked through the open doorway. There were soldiers on the floor, on the tables, on the davenports. Women, black and white, moved slowly among the wounded and dying. I walked up the steps and crossed the threshold.

"Come away with me, Reeves," Mrs. Phelps whispered.

The keening sound was dizzying. So full of pain. So familiar. I knew that voice.

It was Mama's.

She lay facedown over a body stretched out on Mrs. Campbell's best velvet settee. I couldn't see the face, but I recognized the boots. They were my daddy's.

CHAPTER 17

I saw more death today than I should ever see in a lifetime: the blank stares of the dead, their shiny black faces, one lifeless hand reaching out to the living in a wagon piled high with death. You knew that glory would steal life from both sides, but did you know it would take your own?

—Margaret Reeves O'Neill to her father,
August 10, 1861

JUNEAU FOUND ME vomiting in the street, and she cleaned my face with a cloth smelling of clean, sweet lavender. Then she and Mrs. Phelps took us all home—Mama and Lucy and me. Juneau brewed one of her sleeping teas and put us to bed. But I didn't drink it.

I crept downstairs to Daddy's study and walked around the room slowly. My candle flickered. Shadows pressed in around me like ghosts, their voices whispering in my ear, voices that seemed as real as my own. Oliver Twist. Elizabeth Bennet and Mr. Darcy. Mr. Harding and his beloved daughter Eleanor. All the characters from all the books Daddy loved so well. The room was just the same as always. Nothing had changed.

But everything had changed. I sank into the chair behind Daddy's desk, and lighted the big lamp. Its warm glow cut through the darkness like a butter knife. If only I could call back time; if only I could call back yesterday. Surely there was a way to walk backward through the day and snatch Daddy home to safety, to call back the bullet that had pierced his heart. Why did time move forward like this?

I reached for Daddy's favorite pen and for the first time, it felt like it fit my hand. I took out my diary and began to write.

I wrote and wrote and wrote—one long, last letter to Daddy. I wrote about what I'd seen that day, all the nightmare sights and sounds and smells. But I wrote, too, about happier times. About birthdays and Christmases and books we'd shared. I even wrote about Percival Wilder and the fluttery way he made me feel. I wrote until I couldn't write another word, until all the words inside my head had exploded like spent artillery shells. Finally, I closed my diary and put out the light.

I WOKE at dawn. A heavy, thudding noise came from the front hall. Then a shadow flickered past the open doorway. Slowly, I got to my feet. *Daddy was dead.* Nothing would ever be the same. I took a deep breath and reeled toward the doorway.

Hector and Captain Brown were staggering through the front door, carrying Mrs. Brown's big green trunk on their shoulders. Moments later, wagon wheels sounded on the driveway, and the Browns were gone, retreating north with the Federal army.

I slipped back into Daddy's study, relieved that I would never have to see Mrs. Brown again or look into her steely eyes, so hard and cold and insincere.

Then I noticed Daddy's desk. My diary was open, and the pages I'd written the night before had been ripped away. Slowly, methodically, I searched the desk, the study, the hall. But those pages were gone, gone as surely as Daddy himself.

My hands shook as I locked the study door behind me. They were shaking still when I sank on the steps in the front hall. And then I began to cry. For Daddy, for Mama, for Lucy and me—for everything we had lost.

CHAPTER 18

The brilliant victory thus achieved upon this hard-fought field was won only by the most determined bravery and distinguished gallantry of the combined armies, which fought nobly . . . with as much courage and constancy as were ever exhibited upon any battle-field. . . .

This great victory was dearly bought by the blood of many a skillful officer and brave man.

— General Sterling Price, Confederate Army,
Springfield, Missouri,
August 1861

THE STENCH OF rotting flesh rolled up from the battlefield and hung heavy in the air. Lucy cried and said we couldn't bury Daddy, not when the whole wide world smelled like the Devil's Kingdom itself. But we had no choice. The day was hot and getting hotter.

Daddy's cedar coffin was lowered into a grave under the willow by the pond. Juneau led us in his favorite hymn: "On Jordan's stormy banks I stand / And cast a wishful eye. . . ." But my voice was gone.

Congressman Phelps, just back from St. Louis, read a message of condolence from General Price. "This great victory was dearly bought by the blood of many a skillful officer and brave man. I salute a fellow gentleman from Virginia."

One of the general's aides stepped toward us and gave Mama the flag from Daddy's regiment, its yellow silk charred and shredded from gunfire.

"Thank you, Lieutenant." Mama's voice was clear and steady. "We will treasure this always." Then Juneau guided Lucy and Mama back inside.

I stayed behind, unwilling to leave Daddy to the darkness of the grave. Mrs. Campbell wrapped me in her arms. Mrs. Phelps kissed my cheek. Their tender sympathies touched off another wave of tears, and Mrs. Phelps led me away from the other mourners, out past Daddy's willow.

"What a joyless day for all of us, Rebel or Yankee," she said gently, her voice suddenly thick. "So many friends gone. Your daddy and General Lyon shot dead. Young Percival Wilder, missing in action."

"Whatever do you mean?"

"Oh, dear God," Mrs. Phelps pulled away, her voice shaking. "I thought you knew. Why, Mr. Phelps himself assured me that—"

"Has no one seen him?"

"Not since General Lyon was killed."

It was suddenly hard to breathe, hard to take in that foul, ugly air.

Mrs. Phelps rushed on. "It's probably nothing to worry about, Margaret Reeves. So many Federal soldiers went miss-

ing in the retreat to St. Louis. Please, don't worry yourself."
She folded me in her arms, her hands smoothed my hair.
"He'll be fine, sweet pea. You wait and see."

I backed away, trying to ignore the dread squeezing the
life from my heart. Surely Mrs. Phelps was right. This very
minute, Percival was sitting under a sycamore, pressing a
lock of hair into an envelope addressed to me. But the picture faded.

"Why don't you come on inside now, Reeves? Get yourself
out of this air," she whispered.

I shook my head.

"I'm sorry, Reeves. So very sorry. But you must have faith.
Promise me that."

I promised her nothing.

Then Mrs. Phelps motioned to the field hands, who'd
been enlisted as grave diggers for the day. "Come back after
lunchtime," she said to them. "Give Miss Reeves some time
alone with her grief."

I STARED down at the plain cedar box. "Someday, when all of
this is over," he'd said, "perhaps voices like yours will find
some meaning in it." I closed my eyes, and in my memory,
there he was—Daddy, staring out across Wilson's Creek at
acres and acres of soldiers, men like himself, men like Percival Wilder, who could die at any moment.

Waves of darkness pulsed through my veins like poison.
There was no meaning to this war. No good would ever come

of it. Daddy was dead, and I felt certain Percival was gone, too. I would never see him again, never feel his hands reaching around my waist, his lips brushing against mine.

I reached deep into my pocket and pulled out my notebook. How little I'd ever known about life. I tossed the notebook into the grave, and it landed with a dull thud.

I WALKED AWAY as fast as I could—away from the pond, away from the grave, to Daddy's horse barn. It smelled warm and dusty and full of life. Sunlight streamed down through the loft and made the barn glow like heaven. One of the carriage horses nickered softly. I pushed back my hoops and climbed the ladder to the loft. That's where I found Hector, holding a book in his hands.

"Your daddy gave this to me one Christmas," he said quietly. "It changed everything for me." His eyes burned with the same passion for beautiful words and language that had once burned in my own. "There's comfort in words, Miss Reeves."

He held the book out to me, a thin volume bound in dark brown. The page was open to "Sleep and Poetry," and the passage Percival Wilder had read to me was underlined:

> *And can I ever bid these joys farewell?*
> *Yes, I must pass them for a nobler life. . . .*

Tears blurred the rest.

"Words can't raise the dead." I snapped the book shut and handed it to Hector. Then I said something truly mean. "The grave diggers need an extra hand. You better run along now and help them."

Hector got to his feet slowly. I dared not look him in the eye.

CHAPTER 19

The property, real and personal, of all persons in the
State of Missouri who shall take up arms against the
United States, or who shall be directly proven to have
taken an active part with their enemies in the field is
declared to be confiscated to the public use, and their
slaves, if any they have, are hereby declared freemen.
 —Major General John C. Frémont, U.S. Army,
 August 30, 1861

THE FOLLOWING DAYS unfolded like a long nightmare in a
fever: Juneau boiling all our clothes in a big pot of black dye;
Hector reading poetry beside Daddy's grave; Lucy sleeping
with the tattered yellow flag under her pillow. Mostly I
remember the smell of the dead and dying that wouldn't go
away, that reminded us constantly of all we'd lost. Before
bedtime every night, I'd stare out at the darkness, wondering what death was like and hoping that Percival Wilder
didn't already know.

LONG AFTER that first week, Mama kept to her bed, so I
helped Juneau manage all our daily affairs. But I never
went near Daddy's study, nor did I concern myself with the

missing pages in my diary. For I had more important matters to attend to: Hiram had not returned from the battlefield.

Every morning, I'd send Hector out to all the hospitals and prisoner-of-war camps. But he always came back alone. We had to assume that Hiram had either run away or died in the fighting. And there was no news of Percival Wilder. I tried hard not to think that Percival and Hiram might have shared the same fate, that they'd been dumped into one of those mass graves at Wilson's Creek, where already scavengers were collecting battle souvenirs. But at night, when the dry August winds blew up from the battleground, I couldn't hold back my fears.

Toward the end of August, I began to venture away from home. In the heat of the day when the stench from the battlefield was unbearable, I'd saddle Mama's mare Esmie and spur her north, riding hard to outrace the memories, to find just one spot in Greene County where the air was free from decay. But even the Bessie Branch smelled of death.

So I'd race back home and shut myself up inside the horse barn, where the soft, warm, living bodies of Daddy's horses rolled back the smell of death. There, I could almost forget.

That's where Mr. Junius Campbell found me on the last day of August, up in the loft, buried in a mound of sweet-smelling hay.

"Margaret Reeves!" he called. "Margaret Reeves, are you in here?"

I held my breath, hoping he'd go away. Then I remembered that he was a Union man—with contacts in St. Louis! I jumped to my feet, brushing hay from my dyed black dress, and shimmied down the ladder. The moment I looked into his face, I knew I should have stayed put.

"You have news," I whispered.

Mr. Campbell's face softened. "I haven't heard a word about Hiram or that young officer, Margaret Reeves. But I do have news." He held out a copy of the *Springfield Journal* and pointed to an article on the front page. "It seems General Frémont up in St. Louis has freed all the slaves that belong to Southern sympathizers."

I took the newspaper from his hand and moved toward the open door, where the light was better. There was no doubt about the General's intention: *". . . their slaves, if any they have, are hereby declared freemen."*

"Why have you brought this to my attention, Mr. Campbell?" I asked. "General Price's men occupy Springfield and aren't about to comply with General Frémont's orders. And as you know, my daddy has always intended to free our people. I do believe it's in his will."

My words hung in the air like yesterday's laundry, and I knew then and there that Mr. Campbell had come about the will. He glanced down at his dusty brown boots, refusing to look me in the eye.

"You want me to speak to Mama, then?" I asked.

Mr. Campbell turned and stared up at the house. People found it awkward to talk to me about business, but since Mama was grieving, who else could they talk to? It even seemed to pain Mama, perhaps her most of all.

"I have something that needs saying," she'd told me last week, and I'd sunk down on the edge of her bed, my legs and arms all atremble.

"Reeves," she'd said, "I know this will be a great disappointment to you, but I've decided not to send you back to the Fayetteville Ladies' Institute next month."

Then, before I could stop her, she was gushing on about all the parties and balls and dances I'd miss. How sorry she was that all my fine clothes had gone into Juneau's pot of black dye. "Just look at you," she'd cried, tears running down her cheeks, "sixteen next month and already looking for all the world like a widow."

And here was Mr. Campbell, acting just as remorseful. At last, he spoke. "Tell your Mama that we can delay the reading of the will no longer. What your daddy has done . . ." He broke off suddenly, cleared his throat, and started again. "Tell your Mama that it's in all your best interests to read the will before there's more talk about this proclamation."

As he hurried away, Hector came around the corner of the barn and began to read the newspaper Mr. Campbell had left behind. "Looks like I'm a free man," he said, folding the newspaper under his arm.

CHAPTER 20

I have entrusted Hiram with my life on so many occasions that they are beyond reckoning. He is my most loyal and trusted companion. Would this be so if he were a freeman? Still, I have no doubt but that he will find a way to deliver this safely into your keeping, no matter what tomorrow holds for me.

—Gaylen O'Neill to his daughter,
August 9, 1861

"HAVE YOU SEEN THIS, Reeves?" Lucy whispered as I entered Mama's bedroom moments later. The two of them were propped up in bed, a copy of the *Springfield Journal* in their laps. The room was unnaturally stuffy and hot; every upstairs window was closed against the battlefield air.

I nodded. "Mr. Campbell just told me about it."

"Is it serious?" Mama asked. Her eyes were still puffy and red from weeks of weeping; her golden hair tumbled loose around her shoulders.

"Some of our people have already heard the news, Mama," I said. "Hector believes he's a free man."

"Then we could lose everything," Mama whispered.

Lucy's face went pale. "Oh, Mama, please tell me it isn't so!" She began to cry and Mama drew her closer. "Mrs.

Brown—" Lucy swallowed hard. "She told me this would happen. That the Yankees would come and free all the slaves and bring us to our knees."

"Hush, Lucy." I stroked her hair, all soft and wavy like Mama's. "We've always known Daddy planned to free our people someday. It's just going to happen sooner rather than later."

Lucy broke away from Mama. "But don't you see, Reeves?" she cried. "We'll be ruined. We'll have to move away from home and sell all our things. Because if a boy like Hector is worth fifteen hundred dollars, and we have twenty-eight negroes—"

I shivered. "Where did you learn to talk this way?"

Lucy's voice was suddenly strong and sure. "Why, isn't it common knowledge, Reeves?" Her eyes shone with unnatural brightness. "Mrs. Brown told me that negroes are worth money just like corn or tobacco or Daddy's plantation pacers. Why, she helped me calculate just how much everybody was worth, and it came to well over thirty thousand—"

"Daddy would have whipped you with a willow switch to hear you talk like that."

"That's enough! " Mama looked at me over the top of Lucy's ringlets—that fiery, withering look she used to reserve for Daddy when they argued over his will. "Your little sister may have spoken indelicately, but she is right, Margaret Reeves. We could lose everything if our people take it into their heads that they're free."

"But Mama, that's why Mr. Campbell came to see us today. He believes we should read Daddy's will right away."

Mama pressed a handkerchief against her forehead, then Lucy's. She refused to look at me.

"We can't ignore his will," I continued. "Mr. Campbell says it's in our interest, *all* our interests, to read it now."

Mama's eyes widened. "All our interests? Were those his exact words, Margaret Reeves? Remember carefully."

An awful chill crept into my heart.

"Answer me, Reeves."

Slowly, I replied. "Those where his exact words, Mama."

It was then that we realized Juneau was standing in the doorway, and that she had probably heard every single word. But not one emotion flickered across her face. She just looked straight at Mama and said, "I think you better come downstairs, Miz Vashti."

I SHOT DOWN the back stairs, into the kitchen, and headlong into Hiram.

Hiram!

Standing in the kitchen, drinking milk from a tin cup. Milk splattered across the floor, but neither of us cared. He scooped me into his big, strong arms and hugged me tight.

"Precious child," he murmured. "It's good to be home."

"Do you know about Daddy?" I whispered.

"Yes, honey, I know."

There was a clatter on the stairs, and Lucy jumped into

Hiram's arms. "Sweet pea!" he shouted, laughing and crying at the same time. He whirled her around and around, like he used to do when she was no bigger than a mite. Then he stopped.

Mama stood on the landing.

Hiram set Lucy down and walked toward Mama, his hands out. She took them in hers. "Are you hurt?" she asked.

His clothes were dusty, splattered with dried mud and dark, murky splotches of old blood.

"No, Miz Vashti." His eyes filled with tears. "Not one bit. But Mista Gaylen . . ." He wiped his eyes with a dusty handkerchief and I poured him another cup of milk.

"What took you so long to come home?" Juneau asked.

"Too many soldiers on the road."

"Then there are others like you? Survivors, I mean." For the first time since Daddy died, I felt a glimmer of hope. If Hiram could come back, Percival Wilder could, too.

Hiram put his cup aside. "Lots of soldiers still on the road, Miz Reeves. Bushwackers. Jayhawkers. So many I feared they'd steal Mista Gaylen's horse right out from under me."

"You brought Trooper home?" Lucy asked.

Under her breath, Mama quoted Scripture. "Well done, thou good and faithful servant."

"Brought somethin' else, too," Hiram reached into his pocket and pulled out a packet of letters, stiff and stained with dried blood. Daddy's blood. My letters to Daddy.

"These are for you, Miz Reeves."

I fought hard to breathe.

"He carried them right up until the very end. In his breast pocket, right over his heart." Hiram's voice broke off. He began again. "And when that Yankee minié ball smashed into his chest, he said to me, 'Take these to my girl.' Then he died, Miz Reeves. He died. Never said another word."

Hiram stepped closer, his breath warm on my cheek. "And this one here. This one, he wrote for you, particular." He took a tattered piece of paper from the bottom of the stack and held it out to me.

"Go ahead, Miz Reeves. Read it to us," he urged.

"Didn't he write one for me?" Lucy cried. "Or for Mama?"

"Hush, Lucy girl," Juneau whispered.

But Lucy pushed away and ran up the hall, into the parlor. She dashed back, clutching the photographs of her and Mama, the ones I'd forgotten to give Daddy.

"I hate you, Margaret Reeves!" she shouted. "I hate you!"

Then she ripped the photographs to pieces.

I WAITED until the last rays of day shot through the sky, when the house was quiet again. Outside, the air was cool. For the first time, I couldn't smell the battlefield.

I knelt by Daddy's grave and opened his letter. *"My Darling Daughter,"* it began. *"I have entrusted Hiram with my life."* Surely, if this were so, I reasoned, then there's nothing to fear in Daddy's will. Hiram will be rewarded for his loyalty with freedom.

Then my eyes fell to the next paragraph:

I have read every one of your precious letters, and through them, I can see your mama's lovely face, little Lucy's golden curls, and every square inch of home. Your words have drawn a portrait more real to me than the photographer's craft. Promise me that you will never let an army of men silence this voice.

On the Eve of Battle
With all my Love,
Daddy

Tears blurred my vision. I had no voice left. Hadn't Daddy known that if anything ever happened to him my voice would wither like a honeysuckle vine in a killing frost? In the weeks since his death, I hadn't missed my notebook. Not a bit. But now I wondered if Daddy was somewhere, watching me, disappointed by my silence.

"Words of comfort, I hope." Mama laid her arm gently across my shoulders. "You must not blame yourself for Lucy's outburst. After we've read the will, she'll find it in her heart to apologize. Surely your father's last testament will remember her with some token of affection."

"Then you've decided to read the will after all?"

Mama sighed. "I've never believed in freedom for our people. The burden of living would be too great for them. How would they manage on their own? But after today, I can almost understand how the devotion of a servant like Hiram could make your daddy believe that all our people should be free."

"Daddy didn't think of Hiram only as a servant, Mama," I said softly.

Then I showed her his letter.

CHAPTER 21

I, Gaylen Morrison O'Neill of the Municipality of Springfield, in the County of Greene, in the State of Missouri, being of sound mind and body, do hereby bequeath the Land, Property, and Monied Holdings that do rightly belong to me . . .
— The Will of Gaylen Morrison O'Neill,
March 24, 1858

MAMA HAD BEEN RIGHT. The next day, the first part of Daddy's will worked like a miracle tonic on Lucy. The moment Mr. Junius Campbell came to the line, *"And to my beloved daughter Lucy, I bequeath my complete set of William Shakespeare,"* Lucy's voice took on "a far more pleasing sound," to quote from Mr. Shakespeare himself. She didn't even seem to mind that Daddy had left me his entire collection of contemporary novels, a gift that only served to deepen the emptiness in my heart.

"Do you still have the key to Daddy's study, Reeves?" Lucy asked. "I'd like to examine my new set of Mr. Shakespeare."

"You know where he kept it?"

Lucy nodded.

Slowly, I placed the key in Lucy's hand. "It's yours now," I said without regret.

Lucy whirled out the front parlor and ran down the hall to Daddy's study. I met Mama's gaze, warm and shining.

"Between you and your daddy, Margaret Reeves," she said, "you've made your little sister one very happy young lady." Her approval took the sting from my heart.

Mr. Campbell took off his spectacles and rubbed his eyes. "Perhaps it's time we all took a break, Mrs. O'Neill," he said. "This next section in the will is somewhat complex. It deals with the settlement of the slave property."

Mama's face went pale. "Pray continue, Mr. Campbell," she said softly. "I prefer to complete the reading in one sitting."

Mr. Campbell took a long sip of water, then his soft, singsong voice began, *"Upon my death, I do hereby deem that all negro people who belong to me on the O'Neill Estate in the County of Greene and the State of Missouri will be released from slavery and declared freemen."*

My eyes filled with tears—tears of joy, for as Mr. Campbell read on, I heard Daddy's voice instead. His very voice, warm and clear and true. *"They will be discharged from all manner of servitude and service to me, my heirs, and my executors forever. Upon their release, every negro man, woman, and child will receive an amount of two hundred and fifty dollars in gold from my estate."*

Mama sat staring straight ahead, her eyes dry but full of suffering. "How will we get along now?" she whispered.

Mr. Campbell leaned forward slightly. "There is a codicil, Mrs. O'Neill, that changes all of this."

I began to feel queasy.

"What do you mean?" Mama's black silk taffeta rustled as she crossed the room to peer over his shoulder.

"It appears that Gaylen added a few final instructions on the day he left for Cowskin Prairie." Mr. Campbell looked at me over the top of his spectacles. "These changes will supersede those written in the main body of the will."

I swallowed hard. "So these changes are only about slave property?"

"That's right."

Granting our people freedom had been so important to Daddy. How could he change his mind?

Mama's eyes sparkled, full of hope again. "Read the codicil, Mr. Campbell."

Mr. Campbell adjusted his spectacles, turned the page, and began to read. *"Because of the extremities of this War Between the States, I rescind the declaration of immediate freedom of my slaves upon my death."*

The front parlor began to spin. Mr. Campbell went on.

"They will, however, be freed upon the end of the Conflict if they have served my family faithfully and well. Those slaves who are deemed faithful by the agents of my estate will receive a sum in gold equal to their cash worth as of July 13, 1861."

Mr. Campbell continued, and I strained to hear Daddy's voice in his. But I could not. *"This amount has been duly recorded for all twenty-six slaves in my keeping, and monies have been invested with the St. Louis Bank of Agricultural Finance for this purpose."*

It was a compromise. Thoughtful, like Daddy himself, but a compromise still. Had Daddy ever done such a thing? Over and over and over again, he had told me to set standards for myself and to strive to uphold them with all my might.

"Do not compromise your standards, Margaret Reeves," Daddy used to say. "For if you bargain away the values you hold dear, you bargain away your soul."

Now, in death, that's exactly what he had done.

The parlor was so close, so tight, so airless. I stumbled to my feet and headed for the door. Mama touched my shoulder, her face glowing with joy. "I always knew he would take care of us. Be proud of your daddy, Margaret Reeves." She whisked down the hall for Lucy.

"A moment, if you will, Reeves." Mr. Campbell waved me back from the door. "Don't you hold a total of twenty-eight slaves, rather than twenty-six?" he asked.

"Yes, sir. That's right." I said.

"Well, what do you make of this?" Mr. Campbell motioned me to his side. "Have I misread your daddy's handwriting?"

He turned back to the codicil. Daddy's handwriting was clear: "26" not "28."

Lucy waltzed into the parlor, a volume of Shakespeare under her arm. Mama was right behind her. "I've found a minor irregularity here, Mrs. O'Neill," Mr. Campbell peered up from his spectacles. "Your husband's will accounts for twenty-six rather than twenty-eight slaves."

"There's no mistake, Junius," Mama said. "Gaylen's instructions apply only to the Missouri properties, not to the property my father and I own jointly in South Carolina, nor to the property I brought with me from South Carolina upon our marriage."

"By 'property,'" I asked, "do you mean slaves?"

"Yes." Mama nodded. "Your grandfather Cameron Reeves asked Daddy to sign a marriage agreement years ago so that I would retain my property outright. Juneau belongs to me, and because Hector is her son, so does he."

"Then Juneau and Hector have no hope of freedom, other than General Frémont's proclamation," I said slowly.

Mama's voice went cold. "Juneau would never leave me."

But Hector might, I thought.

Suddenly all my queasiness disappeared and left behind a dull, heavy ache. Daddy's will had changed nothing, except my memory of him and his principles. I felt as if I'd never really known my own daddy.

I SADDLED Trooper and rode him as far and as fast and as hard as I could. But I couldn't escape the bitterness in my heart. When I turned toward home, I knew that I'd been right to bury my dreams with Daddy. After all, he'd buried his own.

By the time I got back, Mr. Campbell had persuaded Mama that she should announce the terms of Daddy's will to our people that very afternoon.

"You're more likely to encourage loyalty by telling them all right away," Mr. Campbell had said. "Rumors fly at times like this, and with General Frémont's proclamation hanging over us all . . ." We knew what he meant. If we didn't give our people Daddy's incentive to stay, then some of them—many of them—might leave us the first chance they got.

So our foreman, Bruno, assembled all the people who worked for us, and they stood in a tight cluster around an old buckboard by the horse barn. Mama, Lucy, and I stood off to one side; Mr. Campbell climbed into the wagon and raised his hands.

"As you all know," he began, "Mr. O'Neill was a kind and generous man. Even in death, he thought of you."

Thunder rumbled in the distance, and a cold wind snapped around the corner of the barn. Juneau and Hector stood at the back of the crowd; I couldn't see their faces.

"If you stay here with Mrs. O'Neill and her girls until the war is over," Mr. Campbell called out, "then each and every one of you who belonged to Mr. O'Neill will receive not only your freedom, but an amount of money—in gold—equal to your current worth."

He paused, and we all waited for our people to respond. I looked into the faces I'd known since childhood. Hiram. Bruno. Cook. Their faces were as blank as the pages in an empty ledger.

Again, there was a long, low rumble of thunder, and the sky went dark. I could feel Lucy shivering at my side.

Then Mama stepped forward and repeated Daddy's offer. At last, there was a quiet murmur.

"Of course," Mr. Campbell added, "the agents of Mr. O'Neill's estate must deem your service faithful and loyal before you receive either your freedom or your reward."

That silenced everybody.

Finally, one voice rang out from the back of the crowd. "What happens if we want our freedom now?" Hector pushed his way forward. "We've served this family well." He looked right at me. "We don't owe them any favors."

His words burned hot, for I remembered the day we'd buried Daddy. When Hector had tried to comfort me, I'd rejected him faster than a baby spits out sour milk.

Hector pressed closer. "We're already free." He took a clipping from the *Springfield Journal* out of his pocket. "General Frémont has freed us. Mr. Gaylen's will doesn't matter anymore."

Before anyone could answer, the wind sent the paper spiraling toward the loft. In one smooth motion, Hiram caught it, then crumpled it in his fist.

"We ain't free, boy." Hiram's voice rang out above the coming storm. "But if we stay here and work for the family till the fightin' stops, then our fortune's made. Ain't that right, Miz Vashti?"

Mama was silent. There was nothing she could say unless she extended Daddy's offer to Hector and Juneau.

Big, cold raindrops began to fall, and a gust of wind sent our skirts swirling. Our people waited for an answer.

Then the crowd parted as Juneau stepped forward. She took the newspaper from Hiram, tore it up, and put all the pieces in Hector's hands. "General Frémont cares nothin' for you or for us or for any of our folks." She gave Mama a withering look that told me right then and there that she didn't love Mama more than freedom. But why had she chosen to stay?

CHAPTER 22

Dearest Father,

*Now that I know Gaylen's will regarding our people,
I must learn to manage them with even greater firmness
and efficiency than my dear husband employed. For will
they not attempt to slacken their load under what they
perceive to be a softer hand? Please advise me.*

—Vashti Cameron O'Neill to her father,
September 1861

IF IT DID NOTHING ELSE, Daddy's will served to liberate
Mama from her grief. She resumed her visits with Mrs.
Campbell and Mrs. Phelps, volunteered at one of General
Price's hospitals, and took over Daddy's business affairs. She
left me only Daddy's horses to tend, and my own fears. Percival Wilder was still missing, and our slaves were never so far
from freedom.

For Mama was especially preoccupied with managing
them all. Every morning before breakfast, she'd meet with
Bruno in the dining room to discuss the daily work detail—
who was sick, who was well, who might be hired out for
labor among our neighbors. She took a sudden and particular
interest in Hector and gave him a whole new set of responsibilities inside the house.

Every morning and every evening, Hiram taught Hector all he knew about being a gentleman's valet. Hector would starch and iron Daddy's old shirts, polish the boots he'd left behind, lay out different combinations of Daddy's clothes for the sundry social occasions a gentleman might encounter. If it pained Mama to see Daddy's things used in this manner, she never let on. But it pained me—not just to see Daddy's belongings spread out as if he might return at any moment, but to know their new purpose was to more deeply enslave someone who'd been promised freedom.

How Juneau felt about all this, I couldn't say. She wore that old impenetrable look that could have masked admiration or contempt. But she seemed to watch Mama's every move more closely, and I caught her listening at doorways during conversations Mama had with Mr. Junius Campbell regarding Daddy's will or managing our people.

At about the same time, Mama decided I needed an escort for my afternoon rides. So Hector's only break from his labors was to ride with me. At first, we rode in silence—out past the Campbells' harvested cornfields, across the Phelpses' plantation, or down toward Telegraph Road. Occasionally we'd meet a patrol, a pair of unarmed Southern soldiers on plow horses. The soldiers would tip their hats to me or stop to pass the time of day.

"Nothin' to worry about," they'd say. "Springfield's as safe as a bug in a rug. Why, ole Pap Price is pushing the Yankees north quicker 'n greased lightnin'."

Then they'd move on, leaving Hector and me to our silence. Never had riding been so comfortless.

Finally, just before my birthday, we rode out to the old dairy barn where Hector had helped me hide the best of Daddy's horses from Percival Wilder. It was a fine day. Crisp and cool and fair.

I reined in Trooper on the rise just above the barn. "I was wrong that day," I heard myself saying, "to make you dig Daddy's grave."

Hector's face was a mask, like his mama's.

"Perhaps, if you read that poem to me now . . ."

Hector turned. "There *is* comfort in words, Miss Reeves, but you'll have to find that out for yourself."

A cold wind whipped up the hill. Neither of us moved away. Our horses stood side by side, and together we watched a storm cloud eat away at the sky.

Finally Hector spoke again. "I'm sorry that Mr. Wilder's missing," he said. "He's the one who needs to read you that poem, Miss Reeves."

Hector didn't wait for my reply but spurred Titania down the hill.

CHAPTER 23

O, much I fear some ill unlucky thing.
—William Shakespeare, *Romeo and Juliet*

THE RAIN SET IN just as soon as Hector and I reached the barn. We were so late that supper was already laid out in the dining room. Juneau helped me wipe the dust off my riding habit, then I went down to eat.

Outside, the rain fell hard and heavy. Mama scolded Lucy for bringing Shakespeare to the supper table with her. A lifetime ago, it had been me Mama scolded for reading at table. I smiled at Lucy, but she didn't notice. She gulped down her food, scooped up her book, and ran across the hall to Daddy's study.

When I came out of the dining room, she was waiting for me. "Listen to this, Reeves!" Lucy whispered. "It's the most romantical writing in the whole world!"

She dragged me through the study door and pushed me into Daddy's leather settee. I'd avoided this room and all its contents since the night he died. But somehow being together with Lucy on a cold, rainy night, there in Daddy's study, seemed just right.

" '*Tis but thy name that is my enemy,*" Lucy read in a whisper. She clasped her throat and pretended the high, leather arm chair was her balcony. "*Thou art thyself, though not a Montague.*" She shifted her weight and sighed deeply.

> "*What's Montague? It is nor hand, nor foot,*
> *Nor arm, nor face, nor any other part*
> *Belonging to a man.*"

It was romantical, despite Lucy's melodramatic reading— or maybe because of her reading. For the first time since Daddy's death, words wove their old magic around my heart.

"*With love's light wings did I o'erperch these walls. . . .*" Lucy deepened her voice and swaggered toward me, a tiny Romeo in black petticoats. "*For stony limits cannot hold love out . . .*"

I heard a knock at the front door and recognized Hiram's greeting to Mrs. Phelps. Lucy read on, her voice now sweet and light, the perfect Juliet.

> "*My bounty is as boundless as the sea,*
> *My love as deep; the more I give to thee,*
> *The more I have, for both are infinite.*"

Then there were more voices in the hallway. A man's voice, deep and rumbly. Mama threw open the study door.

How pale was her face, how sad! And then I saw Mrs. Phelps, her eyes puffy and red from weeping.

"Reeves, my precious Reeves," Mama choked. "I fear . . . I fear . . ." Weakly, she held out a calling card. The printing on the card swam in front of my eyes.

LANCELOT S. WILDER.

A man stepped out of the shadows and took my hand. "I bear sad news, Miss O'Neill," he said.

WE SAT QUIETLY on Daddy's settee—Mama, Lucy, Mrs. Phelps, and me—as Mr. Wilder told us his story. My heart was too full for weeping, for I had known all along that Percival was gone, from the moment I first knew he was missing.

He had been wounded at Wilson's Creek, so Mr. Lancelot Wilder said, and placed in one of those wagons filled with the dead and dying. But the wagon didn't stop in Springfield, as others had. It kept on the road north, toward Rolla, toward the safety of Federal lines. And sometime during that long, hot night, buried beneath dozens of other dead and dying men, Percival Wilder had died. Alone. In the darkness.

"An officer in Rolla recognized Percival's body," Mr. Wilder explained, his voice barely a whisper. "He sent the body to St. Louis, and we buried my little brother a month ago. We deem ourselves fortunate to have been able to claim his body."

How long we sat silent there on Daddy's settee, I'll never know. But I wished them gone, all of them. My friendship with Percival had been a private treasure. Only I could mourn its passing.

Finally, Mr. Lancelot Wilder stood up, tall and straight, with shoulders as broad as Percival's had been. He reached into his pocket and took out a silver locket. Then he produced a mourning ring, made from twisted strands of coal black hair. He stared down at it a moment, then handed both to me, wordlessly.

I dared not open the locket in the company of so many, but I slipped the ring on my finger. Looking up into Mr. Wilder's eyes, I whispered, "Thank you."

When he turned to leave, I realized for the first time that he wasn't wearing a uniform.

THE FIRE was low; Daddy's study was dark. But still I could see Percival's handsome face, staring up at me from a tiny photograph in the locket.

Lucy's Shakespeare lay open, and a line of poetry shot through my heart: *"The sun for sorrow will not show his head. . . ."*

A shadow moved across the study door, and there was Hector. "Shall I read to you now, Miss Reeves?" he asked.

CHAPTER 24

Dear Mrs. Brown,
We are discovered! How could you betray Reeves in
such a fashion! I am soarly [sic] *distressed.*
—an unposted letter
from Lucinda Cameron O'Neill,
September 30, 1861

I AWOKE THE NEXT morning, stiff and cold, on Daddy's settee.

Percival is dead.

That was my very first thought. My only thought.

My mouth was dry from crying, my eyes stung. I twisted the ring on my finger, trying not to imagine how it was made, yet unable to stop my imaginings. Had Percival's mother cut these locks of hair while she was preparing him for burial? Was he lying in his coffin then? I tried with all my might to push such thoughts from my mind, but instead I pictured that wagon, filled with so many bodies, carrying Percival away from the living. Hector's voice came back to me.

And can I ever bid these joys farewell?
Yes, I must pass them for a nobler life . . .

He'd read me every poem in his book of Keats, and when he'd gone, I'd pulled book after book off Daddy's shelves. Shakespeare. Mr. Dickens. The Brontës. Mr. George Eliot. Only Mr. Eliot had seemed appropriate.

Every morning to come, as far as her imagination could stretch, she would have to get up and feel that the day would have no joy for her.

That was my future, and what comfort was there in such a thought? I was a stranger to my old life, a stranger to this room and to everything I'd once held dear.

Much later on that long, awful day, I slipped outside and walked toward Daddy's willow. It was fair and cool and crisp. A sharp breeze rustled through the dogwoods, their leaves showing the first purple-red of autumn. My heavy black poplin rustled against the tall, autumn grasses, and startled the frogs on the bank. They made a hollow, thumping sound as they splashed into the safety of the pond. I knelt by Daddy's grave.

What I would have given to have had Daddy there beside me then, the Daddy I'd loved and admired and trusted. It would be so easy, so comforting to believe in him again, when I needed his memory to steady my sorrow for someone else. I clicked open the silver locket around my neck and looked into Percival Wilder's dark eyes. How well the photographer had captured his image. Daddy would have admired Percival's strength of mind, his purpose of will, his adherence to principles. I clicked the locket shut.

It was then that I saw Lucy, racing toward me from the house. Her face was flushed, her eyes wide. She held out a calling card.

"He's come back!" she said breathlessly.

The name on the card was Lancelot S. Wilder.

HE WAS WAITING in Daddy's study, his back toward the door, a book in his hand.

"Mr. Wilder," I said, trying to control the quiver in my voice, for the way he stood there, he was the very image of Percival Wilder.

But when Mr. Wilder turned, I saw that he was a very different man from his brother. His hair was deep auburn. Why hadn't I noticed that before? His eyes were steely gray, and if any of his other features resembled Percival's, I couldn't tell, for like many older men, he wore a full beard.

"I wanted to see you one more time, Miss O'Neill," he said. His voice was soft and deep, deeper than Percival's had been. "I must take my leave of Springfield this very afternoon. I cannot impose upon the good will of your Southern army any longer. For as you may have guessed, like Percival, I am an abolitionist."

"I didn't know Percival was an abolitionist." There was so much about him I didn't know, and that added to my misery. "We did not talk much about politics," I said at last.

"I gathered you did not."

I could have sworn Mr. Wilder's gray eyes almost twin-

kled. And he grinned that very same grin Percival had
flashed at me when he had ridden past my window on his
fine black horse during those first July days.

"We talked of books and writing and other things," I fired
back, drawing myself up as tall as I could, thankful I was
wearing my boots with one-inch heels. How could two
brothers be at once so alike and so different?

"I didn't mean to offend, Miss O'Neill," Mr. Wilder
replied. "Percival had begun to care a great deal for your
friendship, and my family regards you with the highest
esteem." He moved to the window, and for an instant I
thought I saw tears in his eyes. "You must know that he
wrote us about you." His voice was unsteady.

"We're grateful for the happiness you brought Percival
during his final days," Mr. Wilder continued. "A friendship
so quickly made and so deeply felt must be a treasure."

"Thank you for coming to see me again, Mr. Wilder." I
held out my hand. "Travel safely." I could say no more without risking tears.

Mr. Wilder turned to go, but Lucy blocked the doorway.

"Please don't go!" she cried. "We really haven't been properly introduced, you know." She held out her hand. "I'm
Miss Lucy O'Neill, and Mrs. Brown has told me ever so
much about you. Did you take the photograph that's in
Reeves's locket?"

Before he could answer, Lucy gushed on. "Mrs. Brown said
you were a magnificent portrait photographer in Paris, and
that you led a totally dissipated life there." Lucy smiled and

tilted her head so that her blonde curls dipped forward to frame her face. "I've never met anyone who led a truly *dissipated* life. Have you, Reeves?"

Lucy should have displayed better manners, for Mr. Wilder's face took on the color of oatmeal porridge. Still, he managed a crooked smile. "So, you're an admirer of Mrs. Horatio Brown. Many are the persons who've succumbed to her charms." His voice sounded bitter. Perhaps he admired Mrs. Brown even less than I.

But Lucy didn't notice. She plopped down on the settee and motioned for Mr. Wilder to join her. "Do tell me what you know of Mrs. Brown. I haven't heard a word from her since Daddy died."

Lucy held out her hand, and if I hadn't known any better, I would have sworn my little sister was flirting with an older man. Mr. Lancelot Wilder was twenty-five if he was a day!

"Really, Mr. Wilder," I began, "you needn't trouble yourself with this."

"It's no trouble, Miss O'Neill," he said, sitting down beside Lucy. "For Mrs. Brown has proved her worth in spite of herself." Gently, he took Lucy's hand in his.

"Mrs. Brown lost her husband in an early skirmish at Lexington," he said quietly. Lucy's face went pale. "His horse was shot out from under him. Captain Brown broke his neck in the fall."

Lucy began to cry.

"I never thought she cared for Brown," Mr. Wilder continued, his voice soft and low, "but perhaps I was wrong." He looked out the window. "My whole family may have been wrong about Mrs. Brown, even down to her ambitions."

Lucy's face brightened a little. "You see, Reeves. I was right. I always knew Mrs. Brown was a lovely person."

I joined Lucy on the settee. Still, I was skeptical. "May I be so bold as to ask how you came to see Mrs. Brown in this new light?" I asked.

"She wrote a very moving tribute to her husband, which has just been published in *The Atlantic.* The writing is so vivid, yet natural, that it's given my father pause. He may offer Mrs. Brown a position as a contributing correspondent to *The Wilder Review.*"

Surely there was some mistake. Tiger Eye Brown, the author of a moving essay in *The Atlantic*?

"Will you read it to us, Mr. Wilder?" Lucy asked, her eyes still shining with tears.

"Regrettably, I cannot," answered Mr. Wilder. "I no longer have a copy of the magazine in my possession."

Lucy buried her face in my arms.

"But I can quote from the opening paragraph," he continued. "I set it to memory."

Mr. Wilder crossed to the fireplace and stared down at the mantelpiece for a moment. Then he began. *"I saw more death today than I should ever see in a lifetime,"* he quoted softly. *"The blank stares of the dead, their shiny black faces . . ."*

And then, without thinking, I recited the rest.

Mr. Wilder stood gazing at me. "You've read this?"

"No," whispered Lucy. "Reeves wrote it. She wrote it about Daddy."

I STARED at Lucy, remembering that dark August morning, the pages of my diary ripped away. Finally I asked, "Lucy, how did you know I wrote that?"

She turned away and started to cry.

"How did you know I wrote that?" I repeated. "And how did Tiger Eye Brown get a copy of it?"

Slowly, so slowly, Lucy got to her feet and trudged over to the wall lined with Daddy's volumes of Shakespeare. She pulled one off the shelf and took out several crumpled sheets of paper—the pages from my diary. She put them in my hand and whispered, "I'm sorry."

Blind anger drove out all my sorrow, dried up all my tears. I wanted to slap Lucy. Slap her good and hard. But I felt Mr. Lancelot Wilder watching me, judging me, judging us. The pages of my diary slipped from my hand. He collected them in a neat stack and skimmed each page. The pages about Daddy, my memories of the battlefield, my feelings for Percival. He read until Lucy's whimpers stopped. Then he lightly touched her shoulder and turned her face toward his.

"You must explain what you have done, Miss Lucy," he ordered gently. "And your sister will promise not to scold you for telling the truth."

Lucy gasped for breath and her voice quivered. "I—I couldn't sleep the night Daddy died. So, I got up . . . and . . .

and came downstairs . . . here, to Daddy's study. Reeves was asleep. Her diary—it was wide open.

"When Mrs. Brown came in, I tried to tell her about Daddy." Great big tears streamed down Lucy's face. "But she didn't understand what I was trying to say. So I showed her the diary."

My whole body began to shake. How dare she show that woman the secrets of my heart?

Mr. Wilder reached into his pocket and pulled out a handkerchief. "Go on, Lucy," he urged.

"Mrs. Brown said Reeves's diary was very moving and asked if she could have a copy to remember us by, since she held us all in great regard. So I copied out a few pages for her while she was packing." Lucy paused and looked at me. "Then Mrs. Brown hugged me and said what a good and precious girl I was." She added, "I smudged Reeves's diary so badly that I just had to rip out the pages. Otherwise, she might have guessed."

My whole body felt hot, as if my blood had turned to boiling oil. I wished it had, and I wished it would boil over and scald Lucy clean.

Mr. Wilder touched my arm, and I remembered myself. "You'd better go on upstairs, Lucy," I said. "We'll discuss this another time."

"You won't tell Mama?" she wailed.

"Just *go!*" I said, hating the sight of her drooping curls, her puffy eyes, and the extra black petticoats Mama let her wear to make her mourning dresses less severe. I hated my sister. I hated the way she looked, the way she talked, the way she thought. I could never trust her again.

Mr. Wilder cleared his throat.

"Don't be too hard on your sister, Miss O'Neill. She's very young, and Mrs. Brown is very shrewd."

I didn't say anything. "It has happened before," he continued. "A woman attaching herself to a family such as yours, using their trust to fuel her own ambition."

He paused, and words seemed to come to him slowly, painfully. "As you may know, my family has had dealings with Mrs. Brown before. I don't know what Percival may have told you . . ."

It was then that I realized the awful truth—two complete strangers to me, Tiger Eye Brown and Mr. Lancelot Wilder, knew as much about me and my family as anybody living on the face of this earth. It was a chilling, terrifying thought, for I'd written out my heart on those pages.

"I must beg you to leave, Mr. Wilder," I said suddenly. "Please, let us speak of this no more."

He laid the pages from my diary on Daddy's settee and walked to the door. But he turned and said, with a look that reminded me far too much of his brother, "Rest assured that my family will do whatever is in its power to repair the damage Mrs. Brown has done to you."

CHAPTER 25

Dearest Father,
I accept your advice wholeheartedly. Managing so
many people is a trial unto my soul. Yet even one less
lightens my load ever so much, and I am grateful.

— Vashti Cameron O'Neill to her father,
October 1861

To THIS DAY, I believe Mama was so caught up in the business of managing our property, that she never noticed that Lucy and I were only together at mealtimes and bedtimes. Lucy spent every minute with Little Lou Campbell; Bruno and I brought Daddy's horses back from the dairy barn, so I worked in the stables during the day. After supper, when the house was quiet, I'd slip away to the tack room in the horse barn, where Hector would join me as soon as he and Hiram were finished with valet training. Together, we'd read the evening away.

Our tastes in literature didn't always agree. Hector thought Mr. Trollope too coarse, Miss Austen too subtle. I argued that Mr. Melville's writing was obsessive, and that Mr. Shelley's poetry was like drinking sugar water, sweet but unsatisfying. Still, there remained the writers we both treasured—Mr. Keats, Mr. Dickens, the Brontës, and Mr. George Eliot.

Late one night Hector asked, "Why don't you start writing again?"

I stared into the lamplight. "What do I know of life and death and love? For me, writing was nothing but a childish fancy, like Lucy's passion for William Shakespeare."

"I'd say you've learned a lot about life and death, Miss Reeves," Hector replied. "Still, I don't believe Mr. Gaylen thought your writing was childish, and I know for a fact that Mr. Percival Wilder didn't." He paused. "Neither did I."

In that moment, I almost wished I hadn't thrown my notebook away. But what had I to write about?

THE VERY NEXT morning, Mama summoned me upstairs to her sewing room. She was surrounded by bolts of fabric— what was left of the sapphire blue merino, the brown check, even the pale yellow silk. But now they were all dyed black and streaky, the makings of our new winter mourning wardrobes.

"I'd so hoped it wouldn't come to this." Mama sighed. "That we could save all this beautiful fabric against the day when you could put black aside. But there isn't a decent bolt of fabric to be had in all of Springfield, except for these, and you girls will have to wear black for at least another two years."

"What I wear doesn't matter, as long as it keeps me warm," I replied. Surely our wardrobe shouldn't cause so much bother.

Mama took a deep breath. "I fear, Margaret Reeves, that I have something to say that will distress you, and you are so headstrong." She paced to the window.

"You're spending far too much time with Juneau's boy," Mama began. "I'm not talking about going riding every afternoon. That's his job. But reading together in the horse barn—"

I tried to interrupt, but her scolding continued. "Yes, I know *all* about it, Margaret Reeves. Did you think I wouldn't find out?"

"Daddy himself taught Hector to read."

"But Hector is your servant, not your friend."

"Daddy's closest companion on this earth was Hiram Black!" I flashed back.

"*I* was your Daddy's closest companion on this earth, Margaret Reeves, and don't you forget it."

How could I deny what she had said? After all, Daddy had compromised all that he'd held dear to make her happy and secure. Still, I would not abandon Hector because Mama thought our friendship improper.

But before I could say another word, Mama continued. "I have had a letter from your grandfather Cameron Reeves. He is in need of a valet and has offered to pay cash money for Hector."

"We've never sold any of our people south!"

"I'm not selling Hector south," Mama snapped. "I'm selling him to our own flesh and blood. Hector's a troublemaker, Reeves, with all his talk about freedom. He could turn all our people against me. Don't you see? I can't keep Hector here. I just can't."

Mama reached for me, but I jerked away. "You're going to break up Juneau's family. How can you do such a thing?"

"Hector's a grown man, Margaret Reeves. There isn't any work for him here."

"Then give him his freedom. That's what Daddy would have wanted."

"Don't you dare tell me what your daddy might have done, Margaret Reeves O'Neill! Hector's going to your grandfather's, and that's all there is to it."

BUT THE next day, everything changed, for we learned that General John C. Frémont himself was marching toward Springfield with a Federal army of thirty thousand men.

CHAPTER 26

War consists not only in battles, but in well-considered movements which bring the same results.
　　—Major General John C. Frémont, U.S. Army,
　　　October 23, 1861

"THIRTY THOUSAND MEN! But that's three times the number General Lyon brought with him in July!" Mama stared at Mrs. Phelps in disbelief.

We'd gathered in the hallway—Mama, Mrs. Phelps, Hiram, Juneau, and I. It was still early morning, too early really for callers, even for old friends like Mrs. Phelps. But as even Mama sometimes said, "When an emergency arises, a lady does not stand on ceremony." And Mrs. Phelps was one lady who never stood on ceremony.

"I fear General Frémont will burn Springfield to the ground," she said. "He aims to vindicate our Federal losses at Wilson's Creek."

Memories of Wilson's Creek came surging up like a dark, deadly flood: Percival dying in a wagonload of dead soldiers; Mama stretched across Daddy's body; the dead and dying piled up like garbage along our streets. How could we endure another battle?

"There is more, Vashti." Mrs. Phelps's voice was low and soft. "Mr. Phelps has advised me to advise you to refugee south. General Frémont will not tolerate the presence of Southern sympathizers anywhere in Greene County."

Mama gasped, and so did I. It had never occurred to me that an army would force us from our home. Certainly, some of our neighbors, Unionists and Secessionists alike, had already left, but I had always believed their decision to evacuate resulted from panic rather than discretion. How could anyone leave hearth and home behind?

Mrs. Phelps put her arm over Mama's shoulder. "I've always said I'd never leave my home, no matter which army camped on the doorstep. But if I were in your place, Vashti, I'd leave before the week's out. General Frémont may already be as close as Bolivar this very moment."

Mama sank into one of the hallway chairs. "What has Louisa Campbell decided?"

"I'm on my way to see her now," replied Mrs. Phelps.

"Juneau! Fetch my bonnet," Mama ordered. "We're going with you, Mary. I need to fetch Lucy home as it is. I declare, that girl spends more time with Little Lou Campbell than her own sister. Reeves! Bring me my shawl."

I started up the stairs, but Juneau was already halfway down, bearing both the shawl and Mama's everyday bonnet.

"Eat some breakfast, Reeves," Mama ordered as she whisked outside toward Mrs. Phelps's buggy. "Then you and Hector ride on over to Mr. Junius Campbell's. He may be able to advise us on what to do about the horses and hiring out our people." Mrs. Phelps's man George helped Mama and Juneau into the buggy. "And Hiram, I want you to collect every piece of silver in the house. Bury it all under the smokehouse. Have Bruno and Old Peter help you!"

They were off before Mama could give out any more directions.

I DIDN'T much feel like breakfast. I stood on the back porch, looking out toward the barn. High in the crisp, clear sky, a flock of geese called to one another. Trooper whinnied from the paddock. The horse barn glowed a deep, warm red in the morning sunshine. In the back fields, Daddy's willow shimmered like pure gold, and the pond mirrored the bright blue of the sky. How could we leave this all behind?

"Is what Hiram says true?" Hector ducked outside the front door, clutching one of Mama's silver candlesticks.

"Yes. It's true. General Frémont is marching on Springfield."

Hector's eyes shone bright. "Are there any Jayhawkers with him?"

Jayhawkers. I shivered. If they were part of General Frémont's army, then they'd certainly burn everything here to the ground. But then, Hector's daddy might be with them.

Just then, Hiram joined us on the porch. He took the candlestick from Hector. "Don't you go troublin' Miz Reeves with talk of Jayhawker scum. 'Cause that's what they are, young man. Scum. Burnin', lootin', and killin'. They aren't real soldiers, and they don't really care for folks like us."

Never in my life had I heard such loathing in Hiram's voice. Even the lines of his face looked brittle and hard.

"But they bring freedom wherever they go," Hector fired back.

"Your mama raised you to know better," Hiram scolded, shaking the candlestick. "Some things are better than freedom, boy. Like keepin' a family together and watchin' your children grow." And I knew Hiram was grieving for his own baby, the child he'd lost two years before. "You never were nothin' but a stray dog around your daddy's feet for all he cared about you. Put Jayhawkin' out of you mind."

Hector's eyes met mine, and I knew that he didn't believe a single word Hiram had said. Because for Hector, there was nothing in the world more important than freedom. And his daddy had seized it.

CHAPTER 27

Dear Mr. Lowell,

Beware future contributions from Mrs. Horatio Brown, who also writes under the pen name Tiger Eye. My own son has irrefutable proof that the memorial you recently published under Mrs. Brown's name was, in fact, the work of a young lady from southern Missouri, who wrote it as a tribute to her father, a Rebel officer felled in battle at Wilson's Creek. I sincerely believe a retraction is in order.

—Publisher Samuel Q. Wilder,
October 1861

MY BREAKFAST caught in my throat and I set it aside. In minutes I was back outside, waiting for Hector to bring the horses for our ride over to Mr. Junius Campbell's. It was then that a long, black-hooded wagon, looking for all the world like a hearse, turned into our driveway. Mr. Lancelot S. Wilder was the driver. I twisted Percival's ring and waited with dread in my heart. Why had Mr. Wilder returned?

"You look as if you'd just seen Marley's ghost, Miss O'Neill." He flashed one of Percival's smiles. "I hope I didn't give you a turn."

"Indeed you did, sir," I said, trying to steel my heart against more of Mr. Wilder's smiles.

Hector led Trooper and Titania toward the wagon. "Good morning, sir," Hector said, eyeing the wagon with curiosity.

Mr. Wilder reached down from the wagon seat and shook Hector's hand. "You must be Hector," he said. "An admirer of Romantic poetry, I believe."

Hector glanced at me. Clearly, Percival must have written his family about that afternoon the three of us had spent at the Bessie Branch.

"What do you think of my traveling photography studio?" Mr. Wilder asked, climbing down from the wagon.

"I've never seen anything like it," I confessed, and indeed that was true. Though it looked like a hearse, it lacked the deathly elegance that most undertakers strove to employ. And as for a photography studio, I'd only seen the storefront on the square, where Mama and Lucy had had their pictures made.

"What exactly is the purpose, sir, of a traveling studio?" Hector asked.

Mr. Wilder stared at us thoughtfully, and again I recognized an expression so like Percival's that I quickly looked away, remembering a line from Mr. Eliot's book that Hector and I had discussed just days before: *Family likeness has often a deep sadness to it.*

So I quickly repeated Hector's question. "Yes. What is your wagon's purpose, Mr. Wilder?"

He moved to my side. Mr. Wilder was just as tall as his brother, just as manly, but I felt not the slightest flutter or excitement that his brother had so often provoked.

"War is a wicked waste of life, Miss O'Neill." Mr. Wilder's words came out slowly, thoughtfully. "But unless people see it for themselves, they're caught up with false images of glory. Perhaps my camera can open their eyes to the brutality of this conflict."

I met Hector's gaze. Those had been Daddy's sentiments, too. Yet Daddy—and Percival—had chosen to fight, knowing there was nothing glorious about war. Theirs was a decision I knew in my heart I'd never understand. But Mr. Wilder's alternative—to photograph a war instead of fighting in it—was an idea that took a different kind of courage.

"What an admirable mission, Mr. Wilder," I said. "I wish you every success."

Mr. Wilder smiled down at me, and for the first time I saw the smile as his own. Then Trooper snorted, and I was reminded of my own responsibilities. "Hector and I are pressed for time this morning, Mr. Wilder," I said. "Do tell me what business brings you here."

He reached into his coat pocket and took out a very thin envelope. "My father sends you his compliments."

I opened the envelope and scanned the letter. For a moment, the world narrowed to just those few words, copied so neatly across the page.

Beware future contributions from Mrs. Horatio Brown . . . the memorial . . . the work of a young lady from southern Missouri . . . I sincerely believe a retraction is in order.

Then Mr. Wilder's voice broke through. "My father thought you would appreciate a copy of his correspondence on the matter of Mrs. Horatio Brown. He is an old friend of Mr. James Russell Lowell at *The Atlantic*. They both stake their magazines' reputations on the integrity of the written word."

"This means a great deal to me," I said slowly, returning the letter to his hands.

It was, indeed, like balm to a wound, and I wouldn't be honest if I didn't admit feeling the tiniest bit of satisfaction that perhaps Tiger Eye Brown's brilliant career with *The Atlantic* would be a short one.

"We'd best be on our way, Miss Reeves," Hector said quietly, and I sensed that he was eager to know what news the letter contained.

Mr. Wilder acknowledged Hector but took a step closer to me. "My father sends you one more letter, Miss O'Neill. I must ask that you read it now."

I broke through the seal of the second letter. A single page was filled with neat, black flourishes:

Your tribute, sadly attributed to Mrs. Brown in The Atlantic, *shows great promise, and I would be very interested in seeing more of your work. It is clearer to me now than ever, that my younger son rightly held you in the highest regard, not only for your personal qualities, but for the distinctive voice you could bring to the world of publication.*

Please direct any future essays or articles to my atten-

tion. I would be honored to review them, and if appropriate, consider them for publication in The Wilder Review.

Samuel Q. Wilder, Editor in Chief

This time I was wrapped in memory and could almost hear Captain Brown saying, "The old man must have rejected Miranda's poetry hundreds of times." And here was a letter addressed to me from Mr. Samuel Q. Wilder himself!

But my memories went deeper than that, for I remembered all the joy I had once found in writing out my observations about people and places and new ideas. Then I looked up at Mr. Wilder's face and remembered that I could not call back those happy memories. They were buried deep in the cold, hard ground, as surely as Daddy and Percival lay dead in their coffins. I folded the letter away and tucked it in my pocket.

"Tell your father, Mr. Wilder, that I'm truly flattered and grateful for the distinction he has offered me. But there's nothing left for me to say."

"My father is in no hurry," Mr. Wilder countered.

"I fear you do not understand my meaning, sir. I am not and have never been a writer," I said, refusing to meet Hector's gaze. "The tribute to my father was written under extraordinary circumstances. I can never achieve such feeling again."

Mr. Wilder bowed and gave me his hand. "My family merely sought to remedy an injustice."

Again, my eyes met Hector's, and I suddenly knew what I should do.

"You said once you were an abolitionist," I whispered, my heart pounding like thunder in my chest. "Is that true, sir?"

Mr. Wilder nodded.

"Then I believe there *is* a service you can render on my behalf . . . to correct a greater injustice."

MY PLAN was a simple one.

The next day, Hector and I would meet Mr. Wilder at the Bessie Branch. Mr. Wilder would give Hector shelter until Mama, Lucy, and I had refugeed south. Then Hector would come out of hiding and work at either Mr. Campbell's or Mrs. Phelps's plantation until springtime. For surely Mama and I would be back in the spring, and by then I would have persuaded Mama to abandon her plans to sell him; perhaps I'd even be able to convince her to give Hector his freedom.

"You can look after Daddy's horses while we're gone," I'd suggested.

But Hector seemed curiously quiet as I laid out my plans with Mr. Wilder. Perhaps that's why Mr. Wilder said, "Often, Miss O'Neill, such plans take an unexpected turn. Freedom doesn't follow a predictable path."

"But you'll help us?" I'd asked.

The lines under his gray eyes deepened. "I'll do what I can," he replied.

*   *   *

MUCH LATER that night, I sat alone in Daddy's study. Mama had kept Hector far too busy loading provisions for him to spend any time with me and Daddy's books. So I'd packed up our favorites in an old green trunk, which stood in the center of the room, waiting to be loaded into the wagons that would take us to Fayetteville with the Campbells.

My heart ached, knowing that this might be the last night I could spend in Daddy's study, the last time I'd stare into the fire, snuggle into the comforts of his old settee. In some small way, I thought I'd redeemed the compromises Daddy had made against the principles he'd always cherished. For by this time tomorrow, Hector's future would be safe; no longer would he have to fear a new life in South Carolina.

"Some things are better than freedom. Like keepin' a family together and watchin' your children grow."

For a moment, Hiram's words gave me pause. How would Juneau feel, cut off from her son, passing the winter in Fayetteville with just Mama, Lucy, Hiram, and me?

This choice is the lesser of two evils, I told myself, and shivered just the same. My reasoning reminded me of Mama's.

The study door creaked open, and Lucy stepped inside. Quickly, I shut my eyes and slumped deeper into the settee.

"Reeves?" Her voice was small and thin. "Are you awake, Reeves?"

I didn't say anything.

"I'm certain you're awake," she persisted. "I can tell."

She stood so close to me I could feel her breath on my cheek. Still, I was quiet.

Lucy paused. I held my breath. Surely she'd give up.

"Oh, Reeves. Please, *please* forgive me. I promise I'll be good in Fayetteville." Her voice quivered. "I know you hate me because of Mrs. Brown," Lucy continued. "But I'm oh so sorry. Please, please be my sister again."

I should have spoken up, right then and there, accepted her apologies, and promised to be a good sister to her. But I believed we'd have a whole winter and spring together, time enough for apologies then. So I said nothing, and as she slumped away, the space between us grew as wide as a battlefield.

CHAPTER 28

My dear Mr. Campbell,

Enclosed herewith are my instructions for the distribution of O'Neill slave property during my absence. Only Hiram, Juneau, and her son Hector will accompany the girls and me to Fayetteville. As you know, once safely arrived there, I will make arrangements for Hector's transport south. I trust that you will keep me informed, if the extremities of war allow, on the status of my property.

—Vashti Cameron O'Neill,
October 25, 1861

"DON'T BE LONG, precious." Mama tore out a sheet of paper from her accounts book and pressed it into my hand. "Mr. Campbell's expecting this."

It was a list very much like the one I'd already made for Mr. Campbell, which identified the horses we'd leave behind in his keeping at the old dairy barn. But Mama's list had decided the fate of human beings—Bruno, Cook, Old Peter, and all the rest. They would stay behind, and Mr. Campbell would hire their work out to our Union neighbors.

"Run along, Reeves," Mama ordered, pushing me gently toward the door. "Time flies when there's no time to spare."

Then she hurried out to the smokehouse to supervise packing up the hams.

The morning air was damp and cold and foggy. I wore my heavy pelisse-mantle over my riding habit and my hat low over my forehead. The weather had turned just the night before, and for the first time I felt a breath of winter on the wind.

I mounted Trooper and we cantered toward the south field, where Hector was waiting with Daddy's horses. They were nothing but dark shadows moving in the fog. Hector waved a greeting from the far side of the field, then together we herded the horses through the Campbells' fields toward the old dairy barn. Hector kept his distance, never once riding close enough for conversation. But I didn't mind, for my heart was full.

This time last year, we'd had nearly thirty plantation pacers; now there were barely a dozen. Slippers nickered to her colt. Pearl frisked with Chancery, and dependable old Ivanhoe lagged behind. I wished the day were fair so that I could clearly see how each horse moved across the open fields. I wanted to admire every last one.

For this might be the last time I'd see Daddy's horses together, the last time I'd see them at all. How could we hide a dozen horses from an army of thirty thousand?

"They're a beautiful sight," Hector said, reining in Titania alongside Trooper. "I'll miss them."

"But you'll be back soon. Mr. Wilder will see to that." My voice faded to a whisper. "I'm the one who has to say good-bye."

Hector cleared his throat. "I'm leaving now, Miss Margaret Reeves, leaving for good."

"What do you mean?"

"This is where I leave you," he repeated.

Then I noticed the bulging saddlebags, the canteen slung over his shoulder, Daddy's old squirrel gun, the bedroll strapped to the back of the saddle.

"I don't understand," I said slowly. "Mr. Wilder is waiting for us by the Bessie Branch this very minute."

Hector looked away. "I appreciate your help, Miss Reeves, but I'll pay the price of my own freedom. I'll take it myself, as my daddy did."

"You're going to the Jayhawkers!"

"Good-bye, Miss Reeves. You see, I have to go." Then he turned Titania north and headed into the fog.

I shivered. Never before had my pelisse-mantle provided so little protection from the cold.

I DROVE Daddy's horses up and over the last hill to the old dairy barn, where Mr. Junius Campbell and Bruno were waiting.

"Where's Juneau's boy?" Mr. Campbell asked, helping me out of the saddle.

They both knew the answer before I told them.

"Don't blame yourself, Margaret Reeves," Mr. Campbell said, glancing over the lists of people and horses I'd brought him. "It was bound to happen. The boy's just like his father." He folded the papers away.

Bruno said nothing, but later, after we'd fed and groomed Daddy's horses, he said, "Juneau'll take this hard, Miz Reeves, real hard. Tell your Mama to go easy on her."

I hugged him good-bye. "I will, Bruno. I promise."

Then I climbed back on Trooper and cantered out toward the open road. But I turned for one last look at Daddy's horses. Had they ever looked so fine? My heart ached with their loveliness. I waved to Bruno one more time, then turned Trooper toward the Bessie Branch.

CHAPTER 29

But these new images . . . dispersed half the oppressive
spell she had been under.

—George Eliot, *The Mill on the Floss,*
1860

THE SUN WAS ALREADY high overhead by the time I reached
Mr. Wilder and his wagon. He was standing in the back, a
big black apron over his shirt and trousers, gloves up to his
elbows. "Good afternoon, Miss O'Neill," he said, leaping
from the wagon. "Where's my new assistant?"

The sharp smell of photography chemicals poured out
from the wagon and set off a pain in my head to match the
one in my heart. "You were right, Mr. Wilder," I answered
slowly. "My plans have taken an unexpected turn. Hector's
run off to the Jayhawkers."

Mr. Wilder eased me off Trooper and led me toward the
big cedar where the dipper hung. Pain pulsed through my
temples with every step.

"Perhaps it's for the best," Mr. Wilder replied. "Though
the Jayhawkers are a lawless bunch. . . . Let me finish up
here, then I'll escort you back to town."

I nodded and took a long drink of cool, sparkling water. It washed away the dizzying pain in my head, leaving just a low, dull ache in its place.

"And can I ever bid these joys farewell?"

It was Percival's voice I heard over the soothing sound of the branch, then Percival's voice fading into Hector's. My eyes clouded with tears.

"Are you unwell, Miss O'Neill?"

Somehow Mr. Wilder had returned to my side. I jerked away, embarrassed that he'd caught me at such an unguarded moment.

"I'm fine. I assure you."

Mr. Wilder shook his head. He was not a gentleman one could so easily deceive.

"The truth is"—I paused, reluctant to go on. But his gray eyes shone with sincerity. He was, after all, Percival's brother. He had a right to know. "The truth is," I continued, "that just before your brother died, he and Hector and I came here one afternoon. One fine afternoon—to read poetry."

He smiled a wry smile. "So this is where you read Keats."

"Then he did write you about it."

"Percival always wrote about Keats." Mr. Wilder's eyes laughed. "'Thou still unravished bride of quietness, / Thou foster-child of Silence and slow Time . . .'"

"Actually, it was 'Sleep and Poetry' that touched me most," I said, stopping short, and then the lines from the poem tumbled out.

Mr. Wilder looked down at me, down at Percival's locket around my neck. "Forgive me if I've given offense." He sighed. "But there are moments when I'd rather remember my brother with laughter than with tears." He turned away and strode back to the wagon.

I began to recall all the provoking things Percival Wilder had done—the way he winked and grinned and rode his horse by my window. How he'd vexed Mama with the attentions he paid me. The way he'd made my heart race the very moment I set eyes on him. Mr. Lancelot Wilder had given me back a new wealth of memories.

I APPROACHED Mr. Wilder's wagon slowly, unsure of what I had to say. Percival's open locket rested in the palm of my hand. "Did you take this photograph of him?" I asked.

Mr. Wilder turned, a bundle of photography chemicals caught up in his arms. "He came to see me in Paris two years ago. I took it then." He placed the chemicals on a counter and studied the tiny photograph as if he'd never seen it before in his life. "He was the only one in the whole family without red hair."

It was as if Mr. Wilder had opened a tiny window into Percival's life. I'd always admired that dark, handsome hair. But I couldn't say such a thing out loud.

Then Mr. Wilder took off his gloves and reached out his hand. "Won't you step inside, Miss O'Neill, and examine my studio?"

Had I been wearing hoop skirts and not my riding habit, there would have been no room inside for the two of us. Every available space was filled with shelving and countertops and supplies. But I slipped past him, my skirts lightly brushing against his trousers.

"I photographed the battlefield at Wilson's Creek yesterday afternoon," he said, handing me a stack of what he called collodion prints.

I went through them one by one. Pictures of horse and mule bones, picked clean by buzzards. Shallow graves, mounded high to cover dozens of bodies. Shreds of hats and boots and coats, ragged reminders of dead soldiers. It pained me to see such things, but I couldn't look away. "You have quickened the dead, Mr. Wilder," I whispered.

"But my pictures lack words to underscore their emotion," he said quietly. "That is why I'd hoped you would accept my father's offer yesterday."

I was struck speechless. How could I begin to put words to images as powerful as Mr. Wilder's? And even if I could, I no longer had the opportunity. For then, I remembered. "We must leave right away. Mama and Lucy are waiting for me. I failed to tell you. We're leaving for Fayetteville this very afternoon."

MR. WILDER tied Trooper to the back of his wagon and we started toward town. Already the sun had begun its afternoon decline. Yet the ache in my head and my heart was gone. My only discomfort was the silence that sprang up between me and Mr. Wilder, that silence that comes with new acquaintances made suddenly intimate. I searched my mind for something to say.

"So you do not like Mr. Keats," I said at last.

He grinned. "His poetry is far too lush for my taste."

I started to protest, but Mr. Wilder stopped me. "It's no use, Miss O'Neill. If my own brother couldn't convert me, no one can."

The wagon jolted into a rut.

"Hector and I sometimes argued about poetry," I said without thinking, and suddenly the pain returned. *Why had he rejected my help?*

Mr. Wilder looked straight ahead. "Surely the two of you had a meeting of minds on at least one poet."

"We both admired John Keats."

Mr. Wilder threw back his head and laughed, a deep, warm, rumbly laugh. "Let's change the subject, then. What novelists do you admire?"

Without pause, I answered, "George Eliot—"

"The gods be praised! At last, we agree." He nodded over his shoulder as the wagon hit another rut. "Reach behind the wagon seat."

A blue leather volume jolted into my hand. *The Mill on the Floss.* The title was unknown to me, but I recognized its author.

"George Eliot!"

Mr. Wilder clicked to his mules. "It came out just before I sailed home from London. Her new novel."

"*Her* new novel?" I ran my fingers across the name. It was printed in strong, gold, capital letters.

"Her real name is Marian Evans," Mr. Wilder was saying. "Her identity was only just discovered before I left Europe." I opened the book to the first page.

A wide plain, where the broadening Floss hurries on between its green banks to the sea . . .

A lady had written that opening passage! A lady who this very minute might be feeling the chill October air as I was, writing out *this very minute* a new sentence in a new book—fresh out of her imagination!

The thought was intoxicating, electrifying. For though I'd read and cherished books by the Misses Brontë and Miss Jane Austen, they were dead. And the lady novelists who were currently being published wrote curiously unsatisfying stories about romance and marriage. But here was a serious authoress, Marian Evans. A lady who wrote with as much vigor and passion as Mr. Dickens or Mr. Trollope!

"Keep the book, if you like, Miss O'Neill," Mr. Wilder said. "But on one condition." His eyes twinkled. "You must promise that never in our future acquaintance will you quote me a passage from John Keats."

I laughed out loud, just for the joy of it. When had I forgotten the wonder of laughter, the healing grace of such a happy sound?

CHAPTER 30

Five miles from Bolivar
October 26, 1861 — 1 A.M.
General: I report respectfully that yesterday . . . I met
in Springfield about 2,000 or 2,200 of the rebels in
their camp, formed in line of battle. But your Guard
with one feeling, made a charge, and in less than 3 min-
utes the 2,000 or 2,200 men were perfectly routed by
150 men of the Body Guard. We cleared out the city
perfectly of every rebel, and raised the Union flag on the
courthouse. . . .
　　　—Major Charles Zagonyi, Official Dispatch,
　　　　to Major General John C. Frémont

WE'D JUST REACHED the outskirts of town when the sound
of gunfire popped and cracked in the distance like fireworks.
Then three rebel cavalrymen stormed past us, heading south.

"General Frémont's army must have arrived prematurely."
Mr. Wilder pushed his mules into a brisk trot.

Another handful of rebel soldiers ran by us, this time on
foot.

"What's happened?" I called out.

A skinny soldier in muddy pantaloons stopped just long
enough to catch his breath. "A cavalry charge southwest of

town—Frémont's own guards. What's left of us here is headin' for Neosho and the rest of Pap Price's army." He shouldered his rifle, tipped his cap, then ran down Jefferson as if his life depended on it—which it did.

We rounded the last corner. There was home, radiant in the afternoon light. In the driveway, a team of mules was hitched to a wagon piled high with trunks and supplies. The front door was wide open, not a soul in sight. I jumped out of Mr. Wilder's wagon and ran up the porch steps.

"Mama! Juneau!" I cried.

Hiram met me on the front porch.

"Girl! Where have you been?" He hugged me close. "Now get along into the wagon. We gotta make tracks." Hiram rushed me toward the loaded wagon.

"Where are Mama and Lucy?" I demanded.

"They've gone already with Mizzus Campbell. Had to." Hiram lifted me up into the wagon. "The Yankees was lookin' to arrest her. Now sit still, Miz Reeves, so we can catch up with 'em like I promised."

"May I be of service?" Mr. Wilder asked.

"Would you mind ridin' along with us a ways, sir?" Hiram asked. "Town's crawlin' with Yankees. Why, they shot Mista John Stephens dead on his front porch—and he's a Yankee himself!"

Then I heard Juneau's alto voice, coming from the front hall. "Go down in the lonesome valley," she sang. "Go down in the lonesome valley." She glided out the front door as if evacuation were the most commonplace thing in all the world, as if thirty thousand Yankees were of no more concern than a little thunder shower in May. Juneau locked the front door, turned, then stopped short.

"Where's my boy, Miz Reeves?" she asked.

I jumped out of the wagon, disregarding Hiram's protests.

Juneau'll take this hard. . . . Go easy on her.

I took her hand and looked into her eyes, those eyes that revealed nothing.

My eyes must have revealed everything.

"He's gone, isn't he?" she said, her voice so small only I could hear it.

"He's gone looking for his daddy," I whispered back. "But you can't blame him," I gushed. "You know what Mama had planned for him."

Hiram moved closer. I could feel his kind eyes watching me, watching Juneau. Then her face crumpled in like a wilted rose. Both Hiram and I reached out to steady her, but she turned away and, squaring her shoulders, walked slowly, ever so slowly, up the porch steps, unlocked the door, and crossed the threshold.

I started to run after her, but Hiram held me back. "She did this before when Hector's daddy left. Give her time, Miz Reeves. Give her time."

Back toward town there was a flurry of gunfire, then one last pitiful group of rebel soldiers raced south past the house.

"Miss O'Neill *has* no time," Mr. Wilder warned.

"Unless we stay," I said.

*   *   *

I SAT WITH Mr. Wilder alone in Daddy's study. How quiet the house seemed then, so big and dark and lonely. You could almost hear the silence. Did Juneau hear it, too, alone in Mama's sewing room behind a locked door?

"What more can I do?" Mr. Wilder asked, breaking the silence.

I smiled back. "You've already been a great help, sir."

Together with Hiram and me, he'd unloaded the wagon out front, helped us haul the hams and bacon, apples, and cornmeal all the way up to the attic for safekeeping. And it had been his idea to send Hiram back down to the old dairy barn with Trooper and our mules.

"They'll be far safer there than in Miss O'Neill's barn," he'd observed. So after leaving me his set of household keys, Hiram had slipped away, promising to get word to Mr. Campbell before coming back home to Juneau and me.

"There is one more thing you could do for me, Mr. Wilder," I said. "If you could inform Mrs. Phelps of my predicament." I opened the center desk drawer and ripped a page from my diary. "She may know of someone who could get word to my mama."

I scribbled a brief message.

Mama—Do not be alarmed to learn that I am still home. Hector is missing, and Juneau is distraught. We will stay here until she is ready for travel or until Hector is found.

Your loving daughter

I folded the page in half, then sorted through the bottom drawers, looking for an envelope. Mr. Wilder waited patiently by the desk. Finally I found an envelope that would do and placed the note inside. But as I handed him the message, I heard Lucy's little voice as surely as if she were standing right beside me.

"Please be my sister again."

I took back the note. After a long moment, I slipped Percival's ring off my finger and placed it inside the envelope. Across the bottom of the note I scrawled, *"My ring is for Lucy."*

Mr. Wilder said nothing, yet I feared he would think ill of my actions, to so easily give such a precious gift to another. "My sister and I did not part friends. I want her to know just how much she means to me."

Mr. Wilder nodded. "I understand."

He bowed and started for the door. Then he turned. "Why don't you come with me? You could stay the night under the Phelpses' protection."

Certainly, that would have been the easier path, and I was tempted to follow his advice. The house was so lonesome, and outside on the streets, enemy soldiers might this very minute be planning a raid on my home.

But I knew Juneau would not go. So I said, "I will stay here, Mr. Wilder, until Juneau is ready to leave."

CHAPTER 31

*I have read every one of your precious letters, and
through them, I can see your mama's lovely face, little
Lucy's golden curls, and every square inch of home. . . .
Promise me that you will never let an army of men
silence this voice.*

—Gaylen O'Neill to his daughter Reeves,
August 9, 1861

LATER, MUCH LATER that night, there was a knock on
Daddy's study door, and Hiram slipped inside. I ran across
the room and hugged him tight.

"What's that you're holding?" I asked.

He propped a big cardboard box against a bookshelf and
drew me away. 'We'll get to that in a minute, child. Let me
tell you the news. Bruno's seen neither hide nor hair of a single Federal soldier all day long. Mista Gaylen's horses are safe
and sound."

I breathed a sigh of relief.

"Now Mista Campbell—" Hiram began.

"You spoke to him yourself?"

Hiram nodded. "Mista Campbell, he don't believe there's
a single soldier, Union or Secesh, left in the whole town. But
that won't last long. He says we should leave in the mornin',

and if we don't, we risk tanglin' with General Frémont's soldiers."

"But will Juneau be ready to go in the morning?"

"When her man ran off all those years ago," Hiram recalled, "Juneau was five days in her bed without eatin'." He paused. "But Mista Gaylen, he got her to drink a little water after the second day. Don't know but what that saved her life."

"Daddy?" And I'd thought I knew my Daddy.

"She wouldn't have a thing to do with any of us." Hiram's voice was soft with remembering. "But your daddy, he went up to Juneau's bedside three times a day. Held the glass for her himself. Talked to her, too, I guess. Not a livin' soul but Juneau knows what he said to her." Hiram peered into the cold, dark fireplace. "He was a fine man, Mista Gaylen. A fine man."

He turned toward me and smiled. "What you done today puts me in mind of your daddy, Miz Reeves. That's why I brought you a little present. You run over there and fetch that box by the bookshelf."

It was a long, wide box, not very heavy, wrapped in plain brown paper. I couldn't begin to imagine what was inside.

"Go on, open it, girl."

I tore into the wrappings and lifted the lid. Even in the dim lamplight, I recognized those rich folds of burgundy, gold, and brown paisley wool—Daddy's dressing gown.

"Miz Vashti gave it to me when I come home," Hiram said. "But I thought you should have it now, Miz Reeves."

He lifted the gown ever so gently from the box and held it up for me. "Try it on, Miz Reeves."

The smell of Daddy's cigars clung to his dressing gown and filled the room. It was as if Daddy himself had found a way to come back from the grave. But I turned away. Daddy wasn't Daddy anymore, and all our rememberings wouldn't change that.

"Don't you like it?" Hiram's smile faded.

"It's a fine thing to offer, Hiram, but—" I swallowed hard. How could I tell him that all my memories of Daddy had turned to dust? "There's so much about Daddy I'll never understand," I said. "I feel sometimes that I never knew him at all."

"Why do you say that, Miz Reeves?" Hiram folded the dressing gown over his arm. "You knew him better than anybody on the place." He moved closer. "What's weighin' on your mind, girl?"

I shook my head. "You tell me Daddy may have saved Juneau's life, but how do you know he wasn't just tending to Mama's property, making sure she wouldn't lose money on—"

"That's a hateful thing to say, Miz Reeves."

"He compromised away your freedom, didn't he?" There. I'd said it.

Mama's hall clock chimed eleven, and its cold, hollow sound echoed down the empty hallway.

"So that's what this is all about. Your daddy's will." Hiram turned his back on me and laid the dressing gown out on the settee. He folded it precisely, the way I'd often seen him pack Daddy's things away, and placed it carefully back in the box. "Mista Gaylen, he did what he thought he had to do." He straightened and turned to face me. "He talked it over with me, and he talked it over with Juneau."

"And you decided to stay?"

"Your daddy was a good man, Miz Reeves, and a friend to me." Hiram looked me straight in the eye. "He stood by me and my family through the valley of the shadow of death; I'll do the same for him."

"Thank you for telling me this," I whispered, and started for the door.

"Miz Reeves," Hiram called. "Haven't you forgotten something?"

He held out Daddy's dressing gown.

LATER, WHEN Hiram was gone, I sought out that bundle of bloodstained letters Daddy had carried to his death—my letters. I reread every one. How distant that life seemed now, how easy. The sound of practice cannon fire in July is nothing like living with its inevitable consequences. My own words danced before my eyes, triggering pictures of memories, sensations so strong they might have been real. I saw Mama's face and Lucy's curls as Daddy must have seen them there on the battlefield just before that fateful bullet found him.

Finally I came to Daddy's letter, the one he'd written to me just before he died. *"Your words have drawn a portrait more real than the photographer's craft,"* he'd written. *"Promise me that you will never let an army of men silence this voice."*

I snuggled deeper into Daddy's dressing gown. The warmth of the wool and the familiar smell of his cigars almost made me believe that anything was possible.

CHAPTER 32

And can I ever bid these joys farewell?
Yes, I must pass them for a nobler life,
Where I may find the agonies, the strife
Of human hearts . . .
　　　　　—John Keats, "Sleep and Poetry"

THE NEXT MORNING, I took Juneau her breakfast tray
myself. She lay on Mama's old horsehair fainting couch, her
face to the wall.

"Good morning," I said, setting the tray on the wide table
where Juneau and Mama had always cut out our dresses.

Juneau said nothing. She didn't stir a muscle, and I had to
look hard, really hard, to see the rise and fall of her body as
she breathed in and out. I poured out a glass of water, and for
the moment, I was as speechless as she. What had Daddy
said to unlock her heart all those years ago?

Outside, a cold sleet had begun to fall, and its icy teeth
struck against the windows. "Are you warm enough?" I
asked.

She said nothing.

"Won't you take just a glass of water?"

Still, there was silence.

I left the glass of water on the windowsill, then fetched a quilt from the guest bedroom down the hall. But I might as well have been dressing the dead for burial.

Mrs. Phelps was waiting for me downstairs in the parlor.

"Lancelot Wilder came to me last night and told me of your plight. Oh, Margaret Reeves, you are risking so much to stay behind. Is there nothing I can say to make you leave this morning?"

I shook my head. "Did Mr. Wilder deliver my letter for Mama?"

"I sent it by the Albrights. They left town last night." Mrs. Phelps took my hand. "Don't you see the desperation of your situation, my dear?"

"I will not leave until Juneau is ready for travel."

Mrs. Phelps sighed. "You are so like your daddy, Margaret Reeves. But I cannot fault you for that."

I RETURNED to the sewing room at lunchtime with a bowl of hot beans and corn bread. Juneau was ever so still, silent.

"You mustn't blame Hector for running away," I said, pulling up a chair. "After all, what choice did he have?"

I waited for a response, but none came. So I poured out another glass of water and left it on the windowsill.

SLEET GAVE WAY to rain, and it beat against the window like a hundred drummers.

"We warmed up the beans and corn bread for supper," I said, setting the food on the cutting table.

Juneau remained as still as stone.

I lighted a lamp and pulled up a chair.

"Please, Juneau, you've got to stop grieving. Once you do, we'll look for Hector, or catch up with Mama and Lucy, or . . ." A new idea was forming in my mind.

"If you want," I said, clearing my throat, "I'll find a way to send you north with Hector and the Jayhawkers. Would that make you happy?"

I waited for an answer, but none came. So I poured out another glass of water and cleared away the cold lunchtime tray.

"Call me if you need anything," I said, closing the door behind me.

Hiram was waiting in the hall. I shook my head and we went downstairs together.

JUST BEFORE bedtime, it occurred to me what might work. I raced down to Daddy's study and opened the dark green trunk, still sitting in the middle of the room. Books, Mama must have decided, were luxuries we wouldn't need in Fayetteville. Quickly, I found what I was looking for and ran back upstairs.

The sewing room was completely dark, but the cool silver light of a full moon streamed through the windows. Juneau's face was to the wall, and she hadn't touched her food or water. But she *had* gotten up to put out the light. So I lighted it again and pulled my chair close.

"When Daddy died," I whispered, "Hector tried to comfort me by reading the poetry of Mr. Keats. But I wouldn't listen." I paused. Was Juneau listening to me? "And I must confess that I was mean to Hector that day, mean beyond words."

It's hard to confess the truth, but sometimes, no matter how painful it might be, confession brings its own relief.

"When I learned that Mr. Percival Wilder had died," I said softly, opening the book of Mr. Keats's poetry, "Hector read to me again, and this time I listened. This is what he read:

> *And can I ever bid these joys farewell?*
> *Yes, I must pass them for a nobler life . . .*

But I didn't stop there, with just that one poem. I read until my voice grew hoarse, and the full moon moved across the sky. Hector had been right. There *is* comfort in words.

Finally I closed the book and listened to Juneau's breathing, deep and regular as if she'd fallen into a peaceful, perfect sleep. That, at least, was something. Then I put out the light.

"Good night," I whispered.

When I reached the door, I heard her whisper back, "Thank you for the water, Miz Reeves. And the readin'."

*   *   *

THE NEXT DAY, I took my meals with Juneau upstairs in the sewing room. We spoke very little, nothing of Hector. Instead she asked me to read, and I chose passages from Hector's favorites, including Marian Evans and Mr. Melville, though I myself did not admire his work.

Just before bedtime, Juneau said, "Read me that poem again, Miz Reeves. The one you read last night. Somethin' 'bout sayin' farewell to the joys of life."

When I'd finished reading, Juneau said, "Your daddy read me that poem a long time ago. When my man left me." Lightly she touched the sleeve of my dressing gown, Daddy's dressing gown. "Mista Gaylen was a fine man, Miss Reeves, a man who looked after his family. From the grave, he's looking out for you. My man didn't do that when he was livin' here."

"He just wanted to be free," I whispered back.

"And Hector's just like him," she said, turning her face to the wall.

CHAPTER 33

My scout found me a secession house, where we had plenty of sheaf-oats and hay.

—Major Charles Zagonyi,
October 1861

GENERAL FRÉMONT'S army swept into town the very next day, and within minutes my home wasn't truly my own. I was forced to share it with General Frémont's own body-guards, a cavalry force headed by Major Charles Zagonyi, who had led the charge against Springfield just days before.

"Do not fear, Margaret Reeves," Mary Phelps advised, standing beside Hiram and me on the front porch. "These men are from the finest Federal families in St. Louis. My husband has asked that they treat you with courtesy."

BY MID-AFTERNOON, every square inch of our property was swarming with blue Zagonyi Guard uniforms. The commanding officers pitched their tents down by the willow where Daddy was buried and stabled their horses in his barn. The horses feasted on our sheaf oats and hay.

At the house, soldiers came and went through the front door without even knocking. They pushed Mama's fine mahogany parlor furniture back against the walls and used her elegant walnut dining table as a desk. Soon it was piled high with papers and sabers and boxes of ammunition.

I tried to count my blessings, as Mama used to say, for the upstairs bedrooms and Daddy's study remained my own. Mrs. Phelps had secured that promise from Major Zagonyi himself. But every soldier that passed through the front door, every footfall, every shout, every whisper felt like a violation against all that was decent and good, all that Daddy had worked so hard to achieve. Part of me wanted to hide away upstairs, my face to the wall, my heart open to grief, as Juneau had done. The other part wanted to rage and fight and scream. What right had they to take my home?

For the Guard commandeered whatever food, property, or livestock took their fancy. By four o'clock that afternoon, they'd confiscated the carriage and buggy, three wagons, four milk cows, all six mules, and the chickens in the chicken coop. By suppertime, the smell of frying chicken filled the air, though Juneau, Hiram, and I had nothing but corn bread and milk that night.

Just before sundown, I stood on the front porch. Dozens of campfires had sprung up as far as the eye could see, and I knew that hundreds more were burning all over town, beyond Jefferson Street, beyond the trees, beyond the skyline. Then through the darkness I made out a big dark shape moving slowly up the driveway. It was Mr. Wilder's wagon.

"I'm genuinely sorry to find you here," he said. "I'd hoped Mrs. Phelps would have persuaded you all to follow your family to Fayetteville. I fear the battle to come will be even more deadly than Wilson's Creek."

Before I could reply to such a fearsome thought, half a dozen guardsmen were calling out Mr. Wilder's name.

"You know these men?" I asked.

"Many of them. We grew up together in St. Louis." Mr. Wilder paused. "Had Percival lived, he would have been reassigned to this unit."

Again I felt that great gulf between what little I knew of Percival and what I'd learned of his past. I tried to imagine Percival in a Zagonyi uniform with its elaborate gold braid, the soft kid gloves, the plumed hat. But I could not.

We moved inside. The house was all lit up with lamps and noise and action. I was a stranger in my own home.

Mr. Wilder nodded at the freckled cavalryman standing guard at the front steps. "How are you, Taylor?" he asked.

The guard's lower lip quivered. "Charlie Jamison died tonight. Shot clean through the stomach. Held on for three days . . ."

"I'm sorry." Mr. Wilder sighed. "He was a good man."

The guard's eyes filled with tears. "It's hard to lose someone who's been like a brother to you." Then he winced. "Oh, Lance, forgive me. For the moment, I forgot all about Percy."

I took a step back. Here was a stranger who was somehow connected to me, to Mr. Wilder, and to the sadness we shared. Yet he was also my enemy, part of the force that had launched this invasion.

The little lines under Mr. Wilder's eyes deepened. "That's

all right, Taylor. When so many men die, it's pointless to remember who died first."

The two of them shook hands.

"You'll be at the memorial tomorrow?" The guard's voice still quivered.

"Of course."

WHEN I'D SAFELY closed the study door behind us, I asked, "Did many men die in the charge?" Mr. Wilder shook his head. "About fifteen with Charlie Jamison. Actually, Miss O'Neill, I came here to advise you to attend tomorrow's memorial."

"Whatever for?"

"A big group of Jayhawkers may be in attendance. They're camped south of town right now."

"Is Hector among them?" I asked.

Mr. Wilder warmed his hands before the fire. "I honestly don't know, Miss O'Neill. But there's always a chance."

"Then I'll go with you."

CHAPTER 34

*The once sad little village of Springfield now exults in
its liberation at the hands of Conquering Frémont. Who
but so great a general could reclaim this forlorn Western
outpost for the Glorious Union and the Cause for which
our gallant men fight?*

—Tiger Eye, Special Dispatch,
to *The Cincinnati Commercial,*
October 28, 1861

I SET OUT EARLY the next morning with Mr. Wilder for the
Zagonyi Guard memorial service, hoping to find some trace
of Hector. Yet the minute we turned out onto Jefferson
Street, I lost heart. For the street was clogged with Federal
soldiers. And so was every lawn and porch and alleyway. Soldiers literally hung out of upstairs windows, smoking cigars
and waving to their comrades below. They warmed themselves around fires burning in my neighbors' front yards.
They played cards on the steps of the First Christian Church.

"The army has swallowed up the entire town," I whispered.

We drove on in silence. I searched the crowds for Hector's
face. How could I find him among so many? "You must tell

me when you see a group of Jayhawkers, Mr. Wilder," I said at last, "for I don't know what to look for."

Mr. Wilder's gray eyes looked hard as flint. "You'll know them when you see them, Miss O'Neill."

As we drew closer to the square, the houses were draped with red, white, and blue bunting. Almost every house flew a Federal flag, even those belonging to Rebel sympathizers, including Mrs. Campbell's. What kind of world were we living in when an army could snatch up people's homes as if they were loose pennies on the street?

"For what purpose is the Campbell house being occupied?" I asked.

Mr. Wilder flicked the reins and we jerked ahead. "It's a jail for prisoners of war."

Without even thinking, I replied, "But everyone here is a prisoner of war, one way or the other. There's no way to escape it."

The fine lines under Mr. Wilder's gray eyes tightened. "How right you are, Miss O'Neill. This whole nation is a prisoner of war."

Then I realized that these were just the kinds of observations I used to record in my notebook. I reached into my pocket, where rightly it would have been. Such a tiny pocket, but how empty it felt.

As WE MADE the turn onto St. Louis Street, the mass of soldiers ahead of us parted and a band of perhaps forty men came swarming through, their laughter loud and sharp and ugly.

"Jayhawkers?" I whispered, and Mr. Wilder nodded.

Most of them wore blue coats, but otherwise the men looked like frontiersmen—buckskin or butternut trousers, big slouchy hats worn low over their eyes, bowie knives strapped at their waists. Could such ruffians truly be Hector's new companions? I scanned their faces, looking for Hector. There wasn't a single dark face among them.

We started to pull ahead when a shout went up among the Jayhawkers behind us, and then one voice came through, loud and clear.

"Jeff Davis! Jesus Christ! The Devil Satan!"

I turned and looked back. Half a dozen Jayhawkers had surrounded a feeble old man. They jabbed at him and laughed, but the old man didn't pay them any mind. He just kept shouting.

"Jeff Davis!" A hand muffled the man's cries. "The Devil Satan!"

Mr. Wilder reined in the wagon and I started to get down. "Stay where you are," he barked.

"Are you going to help?"

"I'm going to take a photograph first."

Quickly, Mr. Wilder set up his camera. The Jayhawkers were so intent on abusing the old man that they scarcely noticed Mr. Wilder. All the while the old man continued to shout, as if he didn't see or hear his tormentors.

"Jeff Davis! Jesus Christ! The Devil Satan!" His voice grew raspy and hoarse.

Mr. Wilder took the old man's picture and carried the negative inside the wagon for developing. That's when I recognized one of the Jayhawkers. It was none other than Mr. Clifford Jenkins, who had long coveted everything Daddy owned. He leaned over the old man and spit right into his face. Then two other Jayhawkers pushed the old man facedown in the street. Their curses were as loud as the old man's ravings.

Before Mr. Wilder could come to the man's assistance, three Zagonyi officers arrived. They sent Mr. Jenkins and his men on their way, only to bind the old man's hands and lead him toward the jail at Mrs. Campbell's.

"Another one of your prisoners of war," Mr. Wilder said sadly, resuming his place beside me on the wagon seat.

AT THE VERY center of the square stood a temporary platform bearing fifteen rough plank coffins stretched end to end. Already a band was playing, and a group of local dignitaries and reporters had taken their seats behind the coffins. I recognized Congressman and Mrs. Phelps, the Reverend Mr. Casey, and Mr. Freeman from the *Springfield Journal*. Mr. Freeman sat scribbling away in a notebook that looked for all the world like the one I'd abandoned. Again, I felt the emptiness in my pocket.

Mr. Wilder touched my arm. "General Frémont has asked that I take photographs this morning. I'll have to leave you here." He motioned to a pair of Zagonyi Guards, and I recognized the freckled face of Lieutenant Taylor.

"They'll be your escorts this morning," Mr. Wilder explained, already moving toward the back of his wagon.

Lieutenant Taylor and his companion stationed themselves on either side of me, as if they were guarding the entry to a military fortification. I thought of that old man, bound for jail, his only crime giving voice to his heart, and I felt a sudden longing to break free.

"I don't want any escorts, sir," I called out. "Let me be your assistant this morning. Give me something to do."

Mr. Wilder turned, his gray eyes stern. Then he broke into a smile, one of those rare, bright, radiant smiles that reminded me so much of his brother. "All right, Miss O'Neill. Come with me."

MR. WILDER placed a box of his glass collodion plates in my hands and shouldered his camera, then we walked the short distance to the platform. A Zagonyi sergeant directed us to the back corner of the platform, well behind the coffins and row of dignitaries.

Mr. Wilder wasn't happy with the location. "The light isn't good here," he observed. "I won't be able to photograph General Frémont's party from this position." So we moved to the opposite front corner, where Mr. Wilder set up his camera. Congressman and Mrs. Phelps nodded a greeting, though I could tell by the glimmer in her eye, so like Mama's, that she did not entirely approve of what I'd chosen to do.

Just as I handed Mr. Wilder his first collodion plate, the crowd made way for General Frémont, who rode up on a fine black charger. He reined in his horse right in front of the camera and waited a full half a minute as Mr. Wilder's camera lens captured his image. When Mr. Wilder had finished, the general spurred his horse forward and waved his handsome plumed hat high in the air. A great cheer went up from the crowd, a roar as loud as cannon fire.

It was then that I noticed the boy, riding just behind General Frémont on a horse every bit as big as the general's and just as black. The boy couldn't have been a day older than Lucy, but he wore a Zagonyi uniform, down to its fine gold braid, kid gloves, and feathered hat.

"Is that your drummer boy?" I asked an officer standing nearby.

His face lit up with admiration. "Oh no, Miss. That's little Charley, the general's boy. He's an honorary sergeant. Isn't that grand?"

I did not think so. How could a loving parent force the violent images of war onto his own child? My gaze fell to those fifteen coffins. How many of those men had little Charley known?

Just like his father, Charley raised his hat and waved it in the air. Another cheer went up. "Charley! Charley! Charley!" the crowd chanted.

Suddenly I longed to write a few lines in my writer's notebook, to record the pictures unfolding before me, past all forgetting: the Federal flags flying from Mrs. Campbell's upstairs windows; the old man's wild cries on St. Louis Street; and now little Charley Frémont waving his hat to the crowd as if he alone headed an army of thirty thousand men.

My hands itched for a pen. Any scrap of paper would do. But I had nothing, nothing with which to set words to paper.

In that moment I knew I had been foolish to throw my notebook away. Writing was freedom, my freedom, just as riding north to the Jayhawkers had been Hector's.

I STOOD all that morning in the cold, hard sunshine, my pelisse-mantle like cardboard against the bitter wind. Dutifully, I handed Mr. Wilder his plates as he took one photograph, raced back to develop it in his wagon, then returned to take another. But I ached to write.

Another great cheer went up among the soldiers, and a carriage approached the platform. General Frémont himself opened the carriage door and handed down the lady inside. Her face was screened by heavy black veils. The stylish dark green plumes on her bonnet bobbed wildly in the wind.

"I give you the great poetess of the Western Border!" the general cried. As he backed away, she lifted her veils.

I dropped one of Mr. Wilder's collodion plates and it shattered at my feet.

The woman was Tiger Eye Brown.

CHAPTER 35

Bury my heart with my true love,
Felled by a rebel hand.
Alone, now my grief is a gray dove
That cries for this bloodthirsty land.
　　　　—from "The Lament of War,"
　　　　Mrs. Horatio Brown, October 1861

As TIGER EYE BROWN BEGAN to read in that deep, melodramatic voice of hers, Mr. Wilder whispered in my ear. "Be
brave, Miss O'Neill. Her day will come."

Bravery I did not lack. Tolerance I did. My whole self
cried out to silence her. I was ready to call her a liar, there in
front of General Frémont's entire army. And then she read
these words:

"Alone, now my grief is a gray dove
That cries for this bloodthirsty land."

Though the words were not my own, the images seemed
familiar somehow. They were words and phrases I'd used
myself in my last letter to Daddy, cut up and formed into
new shapes, like pieces in a crazy quilt. Then she came to the
refrain:

"One kiss we shared, only one kiss.
But it was true as the dawn.
One kiss we shared, only one kiss
And then my lover was gone."

For a moment, I stood again on that morning in August as the battle of Wilson's Creek began. Again I heard Tiger Eye's mocking voice: *"For whom do you weep, Margaret Reeves? Is it for Percival Wilder, who stole a kiss from your maiden lips? . . . Perhaps I should write a poem about it."*

I slumped against Mr. Wilder, all my anger turned to pain.

Suddenly there was applause. Mrs. Brown left the platform, and the crowd began to disperse. It was only then that I realized Mr. Wilder hadn't left my side during the whole reading, that he hadn't taken a single photograph in what was surely the most moving part of the morning's memorial.

"Was that poem yours?" he asked.

I turned away. Something inside me was not yet ready to share my last moment with Percival under Mrs. Campbell's sycamore tree. Perhaps I'd never be ready. Was I angry with Tiger Eye Brown for using it in her poem? I wasn't sure.

Mr. Wilder led me back to the wagon. He climbed inside the back, and from the street I could see him searching through stacks of old photographs. Finally he took one from the bottom of the pile.

"I have a confession to make," he said, handing me a portrait.

What a lovely portrait it was—of a young lady, her shoulders bare, a pale lily held out in one hand. Never had I seen such a beautiful portrait; Mama and Lucy's seemed coarse by comparison.

"Do you not recognize your nemesis?" Mr. Wilder asked.

I looked closer. The portrait indeed bore a likeness to Tiger Eye Brown. The inscription in the corner was faint, so faint I had to squint to make it out: *"With genuine affection to my beloved. Yours always, Miranda."*

"Her beloved?"

"I loved her," Mr. Wilder answered. "Part of me loves her still."

"What happened?" I breathed.

"When she realized my family's wealth was not as great as its literary prestige," he answered, taking back the portrait, "she sailed for the United States and found what she wanted in the arms of Horatio Brown."

We said nothing to each other during the whole ride home. Then just as he handed me out of the wagon in front of my house, Mr. Wilder said softly, "My brother had better judgment than I at his age."

And I was glad when he drove away, for my face was burning like a thousand hot irons.

I DID NOT, at the time, think it unusual that the front door was wide open, or that the house was as silent as a graveyard. I only knew I wanted to be alone with my thoughts. I peeled off my bonnet and pelisse-mantle, and moved like a sleep-walker toward Daddy's study.

There, I jolted awake.

Tiger Eye Brown was sitting on Daddy's settee, holding my open diary in her hands.

"What a pity, Margaret Reeves, that you've not written a single word since that fateful night when your daddy died." She tossed my diary on the floor. "I'm very disappointed in you."

A surge of anger sent me flying across the room. "You're nothing more than a common thief!"

Tiger Eye turned, her eyes glimmering like a copperhead snake's. "I write from experience and observations I obtain in countless ways." She rose and paced across the study. "I even told you I'd write a poem about you and your beloved Percival. 'Bury my heart with my true love, / Felled by a rebel's hand,'" she quoted.

Then her eyes narrowed. "Surely you found my work moving. Or have you traded your affection so quickly for his older brother?"

My skin burned. "Do you steal all your material?"

"I very much write my own work." She opened a tiny leather notebook suspended from her waist by a long braid of black ribbon. I wrote this out just this morning." She cleared her throat and began to read. "The solemn, patriotic spirit of the morning was marred by one crazed soul, standing in the streets and shouting mad, irrational curses at passersby. Such acts should be outlawed, such villains jailed."

"But you missed the whole point!" I cried. "Couldn't you feel his suffering?"

"My impressions of the deed are all that matter to my readers." The notebook slipped from her hands and swung against her wide skirts. "You simply have not the ability to judge the work of a seasoned authoress." She ran her fingertips across the top of Daddy's desk. "Now, we must talk some business."

"What business have I with you?"

"Just this." Tiger Eye strolled closer. "I will pledge on a stack of Bibles never more to harvest material I gleaned from your diary, if"—she paused dramatically—"if, that is, you, Margaret Reeves, will write a letter to Mr. Lowell at *The Atlantic Monthly* clearing me of all charges of plagiarism. Just imagine. You'll never have to suffer through a morning like today's, all those tragic, personal memories made brutally public."

Tiger Eye stopped right in front of me and smiled. "I happen to have his address with me now." She pressed a slip of paper into my hand.

"Miz Reeves has no business with the likes of you." Juneau stood in the doorway.

"My, my, Miss O'Neill, how well your parents trained these people of yours." Tiger Eye took out a mirror and twisted a lock of hair back into place. "They behave just the way all Southerners would have the world believe. Loyal beyond reason. Do you beat the spirit out of them? Come, woman, let me see your scars."

Juneau moved closer. "I'm telling you," she said, her voice low and hard, "to get off this place right now or there'll be scars on your back."

Then I ripped that address for *The Atlantic Monthly* into hundreds of tiny pieces. Hundreds of *satisfying,* tiny pieces. Tiger Eye's face went pale; her mouth dropped open. "Write what you will from my diary," I said. "You'll do it anyway. I'd sooner enter into a business proposition with a skunk."

"You'll be sorry," Tiger Eye hissed. But her whole body slumped, and I knew then how desperately she must have wanted that letter.

Juneau and I followed her out the front door and watched her until she disappeared into the crowd gathered on Jefferson Street.

"Thank you," I whispered.

Already, her face wore its old expression, neither soft nor hard. But that was Juneau's way.

CHAPTER 36

The Kansas Jayhawkers, or robbers, who were organized under the auspices of Senator James H. Lane, wear the uniform of and it is believed receive pay from the United States. Their principal occupation . . . seems to have been the stealing of Negroes, the robbing of homes, and burning of barns, grain, and forage.

—General Henry W. Halleck, U.S. Army
St. Louis, Autumn 1861

JUNEAU AND I took our supper together that night in Mama's room: fried potatoes, applesauce, and biscuits.

"Mista Campbell stopped by this mornin' just after you and Mista Wilder drove off to the funeral," Juneau said, pouring us both a weak cup of tea. "He said he himself saw Clifford Jenkins headin' up a band of Jayhawkers."

"I saw him, too."

"Was Hector with him?"

"If I'd seen him," I replied, "I would have come right home to tell you."

Juneau didn't answer. She looked out the window at the darkening sky. Finally she said, "That's why Hiram's been gone all day. He went to see if he could find my boy—and to tell Bruno to be on the lookout. Mista Campbell's certain that Clifford Jenkins will come lookin' for Mista Gaylen's horses."

Then without another word, she went up to the attic to inventory our supplies, leaving her supper untouched.

When Hiram returned well after suppertime, Juneau took the news as if he were discussing the prospects for next year's tobacco crop.

"I didn't see your boy, Juneau," Hiram said, his eyes soft as moonlight. "But I saw a Jayhawker ridin' Hector's filly out toward the Campbells' sweet-corn fields."

I WOKE UP well after midnight, my room choked with the smell of smoke. Rushing toward the hall, I pulled on my slippers and dressing gown, then checked every room upstairs. There were no flames. I tore downstairs, where Hiram and Juneau stood shivering on the front porch.

The night sky toward town was orange, a billowing, shifting cloud of smoke and flames. "It's the old courthouse." Lieutenant Taylor appeared in Hiram's lamplight. "An old man was arrested this morning, spouting off in the street about the Devil and Jesus Christ. Somehow he broke out of jail and managed to set the place on fire."

"What will happen to him now?" I asked.

"Hard to say," the lieutenant replied. "He's run off, and though he should certainly be punished, his is a sad case. He lost his wife and two sons in a Jayhawker raid a month ago."

I wasn't surprised, of course, for in my heart I'd known that some tragedy had scarred his memory. And just as surely, I knew that someone other than Tiger Eye Brown should tell his story.

"Have you a pencil and a scrap of paper, sir?" I asked.

The lieutenant reached deep into his pocket and produced a small notebook and hand-hewn pencil. How right it felt to hold them in my hands. "Do you know the old man's name, lieutenant?"

He shook his head. "He never said, but we called him John the Baptist because of the way he spouted off in the street."

John the Baptist, I wrote. Quickly, I scribbled my own memory of the old man. His wild eyes and raspy voice, his refusal to be silenced.

"Do you know why he set the place on fire?" I asked.

"We may never know," the lieutenant replied. "But then why did the Jayhawkers do all that killing in the first place?"

I tore out that sheet of paper and pocketed it in my dressing gown. "Thank you, sir," I said, returning the notebook and pencil ever so reluctantly.

The smell of ash and smoke swirled up the porch. Juneau placed Mama's old paisley shawl around my shoulders. "Let's go inside, Miz Reeves."

But Hiram was moving like a man in trance toward the edge the porch. A glowing, orange light lit up the southern sky like a giant oil lamp. Acres and acres south of town were burning—down toward the old dairy barn.

"Jayhawkers," he breathed.

Daddy's horses!

I rushed past Hiram, my mind a whirl of fire and fear. The lieutenant's saddled horse blocked my path. Without thinking, I grabbed the reins and jumped into the saddle. Behind me, I could hear the lieutenant shouting at me, Hiram calling me back. But I dug my heels into the horse's flanks and maneuvered past a handful of soldiers too sleepy to stop me.

SMOKE thicker than fog rolled down Jefferson and the distant flickering flames cut a brilliant light through the darkness. I pushed the lieutenant's horse hard. We galloped past dozens of camps, hundreds of sleeping soldiers. Only one sentry stopped me.

"Ain't got no business passin' this way, Miss," he said. "You're riding toward trouble."

"I'm a messenger for General Frémont," I lied breathlessly.

"Since when were girls in nightgowns mustered into the army?"

"You must believe me, private. It is a matter of life and death." I fumbled for the note I'd stored in my pocket and prayed that the smoky darkness would mask what was truly written there. "See for yourself. General Frémont's own handwriting."

"Cain't read a word myself, missy. But if you'll wait here—"

"You'll just have to believe me!" I slipped the note back into my pocket and spurred the lieutenant's horse ahead. Soon the private's shouts faded into nothing.

The smoke grew thicker, the light from the flames brighter. My eyes stung, my throat ached. The horse's breathing came hard and heavy. But still there were no signs of any Jayhawkers. The road ahead was empty. So was the road behind me. I stopped by the Bessie Branch, soaked Mama's shawl in the cold water, and pressed it against the horse's nostrils. Again, I dipped the shawl in water, and this time wrapped it around my face to cut the choking smoke.

Not a quarter mile south of Bessie Branch, I came upon what used to be a stand of cedars overlooking one of the Campbells' harvested sweet-corn fields, all smoky and smoldering. By then, most of the flames had died away, though here and there one flickered up like a lost soul in the wilderness. Beyond the cornfield, the fire had jumped the road and new flames leaped high against the sky. For a moment I thought I heard the sound of distant voices and distant gunfire, so I turned off the road and crossed acres of scorched earth toward the old dairy barn.

I REACHED its charred remains just at daybreak. A few flames still flickered against the north wall, now a wreck of

blackened, smoldering timbers. Not a living thing was anywhere to be seen. I pulled the shawl from my face and called
out in a raspy voice, "Bruno!" Spurring the lieutenant's horse
closer, I called out again, "Bruno!"

My only answer was a chill wind that whipped around the
north wall, fanning the last orange-blue flames. I slid from
the saddle and walked through the ruins. Trooper, Slippers,
Ivanhoe—the horses Daddy had raised almost like children—every one of them gone. My knees buckled, my eyes
stung, but I forced back my tears. Perhaps Bruno was
wounded or unconscious, I told myself, and couldn't answer
my calls.

I searched high and low around the barn. There was nothing to be found—not until I returned to the charred north
wall. There, under a pile of gray ash, was a thin volume of
poetry, its cover scorched dark brown. With trembling
hands, I picked it up. *The Poems of John Keats.* The inscription
on the front page read, TO HECTOR, A VERY HAPPY CHRIST-
MAS, GAYLEN O'NEILL.

A pain stabbed at my heart as keenly as a knife's blade. It
twisted and turned and cut at my heartstrings until I
thought I could feel nothing ever again. *Hector has done this.*

That's when Mr. Wilder found me. He rode up on one of
the Zagonyi guards' horses and draped his overcoat over my
shoulders.

"Come, Miss O'Neill," he whispered. "Let's go home."

I drank from the flask of brandy he offered.

"Can you ride?" he asked.

I nodded but let him lift me into the saddle. The brandy warmed my veins, dulled the ache in my heart. Finally it began to clear my head, and I was sorely ashamed that Mr. Wilder had found me in such a state.

"How did you know where to look for me?" I asked.

"Hiram gave me directions."

As we rode across the blackened countryside toward Bessie Branch, Mr. Wilder told me that Hiram was waiting for us there, that together they'd found Bruno, bruised, frightened, but unhurt just an hour before.

"The Jayhawkers got all your horses. One of your old neighbors, a man named Jenkins, apparently led the raid."

I reined in my horse and looked out across the scorched ground, acres and acres of charred trees and hillsides, stretching endlessly toward the cold, cloudy horizon. There'd be rain or sleet before we got home. I reached for the volume of poetry in my pocket. "Was Hector part of the raid?"

Mr. Wilder shook his head. "Bruno didn't say."

BRUNO WAS full of apologies. "Miz Reeves, I should've fought harder, but they came up behind me. . . ."

"Your life is more important than anything else," I said. But my heart was heavy.

Hiram wrapped me in my pelisse-mantle and insisted that I drink once more from Mr. Wilder's flask. Then we rode fast and hard toward home. But our pace slowed to a walk as we reached the first Federal camps. For soldiers there were striking their tents, packing up supplies. A division moved into formation just ahead of us. Beyond them, a knot of wagons, caissons, and carts blocked the street.

"Is General Frémont preparing an attack?" I asked.

"No, Miss O'Neill." Mr. Wilder paused and watched the masses of moving soldiers. "General Frémont's lost his command. The entire army is preparing to retreat."

CHAPTER 37

And so the Union army retreats, as do our hopes for a decisive battle. But the flame of freedom flickers bright. A caravan several miles long snakes out of Springfield, as hundreds of enslaved negroes seek new lives in Kansas, freed by that glorious band of men known as the Jay-hawkers.

> —Tiger Eye, Final Dispatch,
> to *The Cincinnati Commercial,*
> October 29, 1861

A SLEETY RAIN WAS FALLING as we neared the house, turning Jefferson Street into a river of mud, piercing our clothes with damp and cold. Up ahead, a handful of rowdy soldiers, wearing blue coats and buckskins, fired their sidearms into the air, and dozens of negroes, carrying bundles on their backs, fell into line.

Bruno's eyes widened. "Jayhawkers, Miz Reeves. Ever' last one of 'em."

I spurred my horse for a closer look, and to this day, I believe I saw Clifford Jenkins astride Ivanhoe. I should have charged ahead, demanded that he return my property, but I was too cold and tired and heartsick. Then I recognized one of the negro faces in the crowd. It was Cook—with a bundle on her back!

I reined in the lieutenant's horse and stared.

"Looks like they're running away, doesn't it?" Mr. Wilder observed.

"Sure does," Hiram agreed. He brought up his mule alongside my horse, and we watched, shivering in the rain, as dozens and dozens of slave folk, all carrying packs or bundles or old carpetbags, fell into line behind those Jayhawkers. They were running away to freedom in Kansas. There was no doubt about it. I scanned the black faces for a glimpse of Hector, but he wasn't among them, though I recognized at least half a dozen other O'Neill folk.

So Daddy's compromise hadn't worked after all. Freedom was more important, no matter what Daddy or Hiram had believed. Still, for the first time I began to understand what living without our people would truly be like, why Daddy had chosen his family's security over principle. Even if Mama and Lucy could safely return home in the spring, who would plant our corn and tobacco? How would we survive?

The rain fell hard and heavy and cold. Prickly pellets of ice bounced off my saddle. Mr. Wilder spurred his horse ahead and motioned for me to follow. But there was one question that still needed asking. I turned to face Hiram and Bruno. "Do you want to go, too? Tell me true."

Hiram shook his head. "I speak only for myself. But I'm stayin', Miz Reeves. I told you once, and now I'm tellin' you twice, I'm here for the duration. I'll have my reward when it's all over."

But Bruno, I could tell, felt differently. His eyes lingered on the folks moving up Jefferson, behind those Jayhawkers.

Was it his fear of Jayhawkers or his habit of deferring to all of us that kept him silent? I reached across the saddle and touched his arm.

"Do what you think best, Bruno," I said, my voice no more than a whisper.

Then he tipped his hat to me and rode ahead into the rain.

BY THE TIME we got home, rain had given way to snow, the kind of big, fluffy flakes that used to make Lucy's eyes sparkle. Was it snowing in Fayetteville? Was Lucy calling Mama to the window to watch the snowflakes dancing, like she always used to do?

Hiram helped me from the saddle.

"Looks like most them soldiers is gone, Miz Reeves."

Squinting through the white swirl of snow, I could barely see a few Zagonyi tents down toward Daddy's willow.

Mr. Wilder frowned. "It'll be the dickens finding Taylor now," he said, nodding toward my horse. "And the last thing you need at this moment, Miss O'Neill, is a horse-thieving charge."

"I'll go with you then, Mista Wilder," Hiram volunteered.

So I entered the house alone.

It was dark and cold and silent. I crept down the hall, past the two parlors and the dining room, where the Zagonyi guard had left the furniture in disarray, past the door to Daddy's study, out to the kitchen. That's where I found Juneau, sitting alone in the shadows. She stared at a single, unlit candle in the middle of the table. Tears streamed down her face.

I'd never seen her cry before.

She looked up at me and said, "He's really gone, Miz Reeves. To Kansas."

"Then why don't you go with him?" I took her hand. She didn't pull away.

For a long moment, we sat like that, quiet and close. I could hear her breathing, feel her heartache as if it were my own.

Finally, she said, "It's time I cut the apron strings, Miz Reeves." She looked me square in the eye. "I used to tell your mama that she was like the ivy out front, chokin' out the roses. She was smotherin' you girls."

Juneau took a deep breath and looked out the back door. "All the while, I was that ivy myself." More tears streamed down her face, even as her voice grew strong and true. "Wrapping myself too tight—first around my man, then around my boy. I've got to give him room to grow, to let him be a man."

I BREWED Juneau a sleeping tea and sent her off to bed. Through the kitchen window, one lone cavalryman's campfire sparkled like a glittering gem against the dark, steely gray sky. The snow had turned back to rain, and it fell as a fine mist, soft and tender.

I found a dry homespun shawl hanging on a nail by the back door, draped it over my head, and slipped outside. The backyard was nothing but mud, the lawn churned like butter by the guards' horses, wagons, and mules. How quiet it was, how lonesome. Through the gloom, I could just make out the shape of Daddy's willow. The wind and rain and snow had stripped its leaves bare. But I saw something else, too. The shape of a man, crouching by Daddy's grave.

Hector stood up as soon as he saw me. He was wet to the bone, hatless, coatless. "You aren't going to change my mind, Miss Reeves," he said. "I'm going to Kansas to train as a soldier."

A sharp wind, as cold and fierce as Hector's determination, tugged at my shawl. Hector had every right to go, every right to be free of us all, even his mama. So I said nothing and knelt by Daddy's grave.

"This is my fight, Miss Reeves," Hector said, gazing out at the few ghostly white tents of the remaining Zagonyi Guard. "I can't ask them to do all the fighting, can I?"

"But you've seen what war brings!" I answered. Images of Wilson's Creek closed in all around me. Percival, Daddy, the blank faces of the dead.

"None of that matters," Hector replied softly, pulling me to my feet.

We stood staring at each other a long, long time. Hector wasn't interested in glory any more than Daddy had been, but the war could steal his life away, just as easily. A flood of sudden tears stung my eyes.

I reached into my pocket for Hector's book of Keats. "I found this today, at the dairy barn." Then I tried to say, without bitterness, that as a soldier, he had every right to ride with the Jayhawkers, to lead Clifford Jenkins to Daddy's horses. But my voice failed me.

Hector opened the book and squinted down at Daddy's inscription, so faint in the deepening twilight. "I had to do what I had to do—to prove myself," he said. "But you'll find Trooper and Titania at Mrs. Phelps's place."

"Titania, too?"

"Jayhawkers won't let a black man ride a horse like her. They don't want us riding at all." He paused. "I'll be a foot soldier."

"Is that what your daddy does?"

Hector shook his head. "I haven't found him yet."

Then Hector took something from his shirt pocket, something square and small and thin, a leather notebook. He stared at it for a moment.

"I don't think you should have thrown this away." He pressed my writer's notebook into my hand.

"But how did you—"

"You sent me out with the grave diggers, remember?"

A rush of shame and regret swept over me like an icy wind, silencing the gratitude I knew I should express. How selfish I had been, how cruel and unfeeling, yet Hector had somehow forgiven me, saved a part of myself that I had nearly destroyed.

At last I said, "I am forever in your debt. You have known me better than I have known myself."

Hector nodded. Then he ran into the mist.

CHAPTER 38

Time is not a great healer. Losing Daddy and Percival will be a wound I'll bear forever. But their memories grow sharper, deeper, sweeter; and when I write out my remembrances, the words on this very page give them life. Now I understand why I must never again silence the voice that comes from my heart.

—The Diary of Margaret Reeves O'Neill, October 29, 1861

MR. WILDER WAS WAITING for me in Daddy's study.

"I must leave in the morning," he announced, throwing another log on the fire. "I don't believe General Price would welcome an abolitionist photographer once his army reoccupies Springfield."

"What do you mean?" I asked, edging closer to the fire.

"I've just learned that Governor Jackson's legislature has voted unanimously to join the Confederacy. Missouri is both in the Union and out of it. Now there's no doubt that General Price will claim as much of Missouri as he can for the Confederacy."

The fire shifted and sent sparks flying up the chimney. Shadows danced across Daddy's bookshelves, but they were friendly shadows, the kind that steal into a room at night and open your mind to all kinds of possibilities. For now I felt free of sorrow, free of silence. Reaching into my pocket, I touched my writer's notebook. I realized then that an army of men hadn't silenced my voice; I'd silenced it myself. Out of anger and sorrow and fear. Hector had helped me defeat that silence, and in his own way, so had Mr. Wilder.

"I will miss you, kind sir," I said, giving Mr. Wilder my hand.

"I leave you one last gift," he said, bowing low. Then he handed me an envelope, wrapped in brown paper and tied up with string.

I ripped into the package to find a photograph of the old man, his eyes so sad and empty, in the midst of Mr. Jenkins's Jayhawkers.

"Write out his story, Miss O'Neill," Mr. Wilder urged, "and send it to my father at *The Wilder Review*. Remember, his offer still stands."

I made Mr. Wilder no promises, but I accepted his gift of the old man's picture as if it were a precious jewel.

MR. WILDER took his leave, and I wrapped myself in Daddy's paisley dressing gown. But I wasn't ready for sleep. There were too many voices, too many memories in my head. They came at me swift and sweet and sure. So I took Lieutenant Taylor's scrap of paper from my pocket, opened my notebook, and began to write.

He was called John the Baptist because his voice could not be silenced, not even by a band of Jayhawkers. . . .

AUTHOR'S NOTE

MANY ACCOUNTS of the American Civil War make a very clear distinction between Rebels and Yankees: A Rebel owned slaves and supported the Confederacy; a Yankee opposed slavery and fought for the Union. But loyalties in Missouri and other border states were much more complex than that. Slave ownership, for example, didn't necessarily determine political loyalties.

The real people who appear in *A Voice from the Border* reflect this complexity. Indeed, such slaveholders as Mrs. Campbell and her sons were dedicated Secessionists. Junius Campbell's political sympathies aren't as clear. A Greene County history of 1883 identifies him as a "leading southern man" during the war years, but his own grandniece records that he was the only Union sympathizer in the family. For the purposes of my story, I've sided with the niece.

But Congressman and Mrs. John Phelps, although slaveholders, remained loyal to the Union throughout the war. Congressman Phelps fought with distinction for the Union at the Battle of Pea Ridge in 1862 and secured an appointment as Military Governor of Arkansas from President Lincoln later that year.

General Nathaniel Lyon, General Sterling Price, General John C. Frémont, and the Phelps slave George are also historical figures. But Margaret Reeves and her family are pure invention. So are Hector, Juneau, and Hiram; Captain and Tiger Eye Brown; and Percival, Lancelot, and Samuel Wilder.

Yet many incidents in *A Voice from the Border* are drawn from history: Federal troops did interrupt a meeting at the First Christian Church in Springfield, Missouri, on June 24, 1861. They forced church members to declare their political loyalties and arrested Southern sympathizers.

I invented the incidents surrounding Reeves and Mrs. Campbell's secret visit to General Price before the Battle of Wilson's Creek. However, "two loyal ladies of the South" reportedly visited him on August 8, 1861, and provided information on Federal troop movements in Springfield. Later in the war, Mrs. Campbell actually did smuggle medical supplies to Confederate forces.

Federal officers boarded with several Springfield families, including Mrs. Campbell. And according to the unpublished manuscript of Louisa C. Sheppard (Little Lou in *A Voice from the Border*), Mrs. Campbell actually had General Lyon to dinner the day before the Battle of Wilson's Creek. I'm indebted to Mrs. Sheppard's account of this dramatic encounter.

General Price did provide an official escort for General Lyon's body as Federal troops began their retreat. And Mrs. Phelps and George claimed the general's body, secured a walnut coffin, and temporarily buried it on the Phelpses' property.

The compromise Daddy reaches in his will also has historical precedent. According to historian Elmo Ingenthron, a slaveholder named Hence Virden of Pea Ridge, Arkansas, offered similar terms to his slaves when war broke out.

General Frémont issued an emancipation proclamation in August 1861. President Lincoln's displeasure with this action (he didn't want to further alienate border states and drive them into the Confederacy) was one of the primary reasons Frémont lost his command in Springfield.

Admittedly, however, I've tampered with history.

I invented the friendship between Mama, Mrs. Campbell, and Mrs. Phelps. Even so, the idea that personal friendships continued despite conflicting military loyalties is also based on fact. Mrs. Campbell's Union friends paid her taxes after she fled south and did so until the Campbells returned to Springfield after the war in 1865.

In the interest of clarity, I've simplified Federal and Confederate commands. General Benjamin McCulloch, for example, was actually in command of Southern troops during the Battle of Wilson's Creek, though Sterling Price technically outranked him. I've also simplified and condensed Frémont's final days in Springfield during the fall of 1861. Federal troops remained in Springfield until early November. The chronology at the end of these notes reflects history as it really happened.

The Jayhawker fires at the end of *A Voice from the Border* are essentially fictional, though that same 1883 Greene County history states that Jayhawkers burned and looted several houses during their Springfield retreat. As the war in Missouri continued, such incidents became common.

Jim Lane's Jayhawkers encouraged slaves to join them. According to historian Jay Monaghan, as Lane left Springfield in November, he formed a "Black Brigade" composed of runaway slaves—men, women, and children. Thus, Hector's interest in becoming a soldier so early in the war isn't surprising. Less than a year later, in the summer of 1862, Lane openly advocated a then radical idea: the official enlistment of the slaves he had freed. Although President Lincoln publicly opposed the idea, he gave Lane verbal authority to organize Negro regiments, which some historians believe were the first of the Civil War. The President didn't publicly endorse the policy of enlisting African-American troops until he issued the Emancipation Proclamation in 1863.

I should also clarify the use of the word *servant* in the novel. Slaveholders rarely used the term *slave* to describe the people in their own service. Usually, the personal writings of the period identified slaves by their first names; otherwise, slaveholders usually opted for the word *servant*. I adopted this historic euphemism to maintain the dialogue's authenticity.

Finally, Missouri was both in the Union and out of it. Claiborne Jackson, its duly elected governor in 1861, supported the Confederacy. With General Lyon's Federal army in pursuit, Governor Jackson abandoned Jefferson City, Missouri's capital, in June 1861, taking the state seal and other critical documents with him. Eventually, Union delegates to the state's secession convention appointed their own governor, Hamilton R. Gamble. Although these Unionists had no mandate from Missouri's citizens to take such action, President Abraham Lincoln recognized Gamble and his legislature as Missouri's official government throughout the Civil War.

In the meantime, Jackson created his own "official" Secessionist legislature in Neosho, Missouri. From this point on, Missouri had two governments, and on November 28, 1861, the Confederate Congress admitted Missouri to the Confederacy. By the end of the war, what was left of Missouri's Secessionist government was headquartered in Marshall, Texas.

A CHRONOLOGY
OF HISTORIC EVENTS
MISSOURI, 1861

June 12–15	Fearing Federal capture, Missouri's Secessionist governor Claiborne Jackson abandons Jefferson City, the state capital. Federal General Nathaniel Lyon occupies the city.
June 24	Federal troops arrive in Springfield. Governor Jackson and General Sterling Price gather Secessionist troops at Cowskin Prairie.
July 22	Pro-Union delegates to the state convention on Secession reconvene and declare all chief state offices vacant. They appoint Hamilton Gamble provisional governor.
July 25	General Price and his troops march north from Cowskin Prairie toward Springfield.
August 1	General Lyon's forces march south out of Springfield.
August 2	*Skirmish at Dug Springs*
August 6	Confederate army occupies Wilson's Creek.

August 8	"Two loyal ladies of the South" pay a call on General Price at Wilson's Creek.
August 10	***Battle of Wilson's Creek*** General Lyon is killed. Federal army retreats north.
August 25	General Price's army marches north out of Springfield; a small home guard is left behind to protect the town.
August 30	General John C. Frémont, who in July had assumed command of all Union forces in the West, issues an emancipation proclamation, freeing slaves of Confederate sympathizers living in Missouri.
September 18–21	***Siege of Lexington, Missouri*** General Price's army defeats Federal troops.
September 26	Governor Jackson calls for a special meeting of the Missouri legislature at Neosho in October. Only pro-secession legislators will attend.
October 7	General Frémont's massive Federal army begins its march south toward Springfield.
October 25	***Zagonyi Charge on Springfield***
October 27	General Frémont's forces occupy Springfield.

October 28	Springfield's old courthouse building burns; Governor Jackson's legislature passes Act of Secession.
October 29	General Frémont holds a public funeral for those killed in the Zagonyi Charge.
November 2	General Frémont loses his command.
November 3	Frémont's replacement, General David Hunter, arrives in Springfield.
November 4	Frémont leaves Springfield.
November 9	Federal troops withdraw from Springfield.
Mid-November	General Price and his Secessionist army reoccupy Springfield.
November 28	The Confederate Congress admits Missouri to the Confederacy.

BIBLIOGRAPHY

Baym, Nina. *Women's Fiction: A Guide to Novels by and about Women in America, 1820–1870*. Ithaca: Cornell University Press, 1978.

Bearss, Edwin C. *The Battle of Wilson's Creek*. Third edition. Springfield, MO: Wilson's Creek National Battlefield Foundation, 1988.

Berlin, Jean V., ed. *A Confederate Nurse. The Diary of Ada W. Bascot, 1860–1863*. Columbia: University of South Carolina Press, 1994.

Blassingame, John W. *The Slave Community: Plantation Life in the Antebellum South*. New York: Oxford University Press, 1972.

Brady, Irene. *America's Horses and Ponies*. Boston: Houghton Mifflin, 1969.

Britton, Wiley. *The Civil War on the Border*. New York: G. P. Putnam's Sons, 1899.

Brooksher, William Riley. *Bloody Hill: The Civil War Battle of Wilson's Creek*. Washington and London: Brassey's, 1995.

The Camera. Amsterdam: Time-Life Books, 1981.

Clinton, Catherine, and Nina Silber, eds. *Divided Houses: Gender and the Civil War*. New York: Oxford University Press, 1992.

Crowell, Pers. *Cavalcade of American Horses*. New York: Bonanza Books, 1951.

Eliot, George. *Adam Bede*. New York: Book-of-the-Month Club, 1992.

Eliot, George. *The Mill on the Floss*. New York: Book-of-the-Month Club, 1992.

Evans, Augusta Jane. *Beulah*. Baton Rouge: Louisiana State University Press, 1992.

———. *Macaria; or, Altars of Sacrifice*. Baton Rouge: Louisiana State University Press, 1992.

Faust, Drew Gilpin. *Mothers of Invention: Women of the Slaveholding South in the American Civil War*. Chapel Hill: University of North Carolina Press, 1996.

Fellman, Michael. *Inside War: The Guerrilla Conflict in Missouri During the American Civil War*. New York: Oxford University Press, 1989.

Fremont, Jessie Benton. *The Story of the Guard: A Chronicle of the War*. Boston: Ticknor & Fields, 1863.

Gernsheim, Helmut. *A Concise History of Photography*. Third edition. New York: Dover Publications, 1986.

History of Greene County, Missouri. St. Louis: Western Historical Company, 1883.

Horan, James D. *Mathew Brady: Historian with a Camera*. New York: Crown Publishers, Inc., 1955.

Ingenthron, Elmo. *Borderland Rebellion: A History of the Civil War on the Missouri-Arkansas Border*. Branson, MO: The Ozarks Mountaineer, 1980.

Lederer, Katherine. *Many Thousand Gone: Springfield's Lost Black History*. Missouri Committee for the Humanities and the Gannett Foundation, 1986.

Meyer, Duane. *The Heritage of Missouri: A History*. St. Louis: State Publishing Company, 1973.

Monaghan, Jay. *Civil War on the Western Border 1854–1865.* New York: Bonanza Books, 1955.

Moss, Elizabeth. *Domestic Novelists in the Old South: Defenders of Southern Culture.* Baton Rouge: Louisiana State University Press, 1992.

Murphy, Jim. *The Boys' War: Confederate and Union Soldiers Talk About the Civil War.* New York: Clarion Books, 1990.

Rosenblum, Naomi. *A World History of Photography.* Third edition. New York, London, Paris: Abbeville Press, 1997.

Schwartz, Gerald, ed. *A Woman Doctor's Civil War, Esther Hill Hawks' Diary.* Columbia: University of South Carolina Press, 1984.

Self, Margaret Cabell. *Horses of Today.* New York: Duell, Sloan, & Pearce, 1964.

Shaara, Michael. *The Killer Angels.* NY: David McKay Company, Inc., 1974.

Shakespeare, William. *The Complete Works of William Shakespeare.* Ed. William Aldis Wright. The Cambridge Edition Text. Garden City, NY: Doubleday & Company, 1936.

Sheppard, Louisa C. *A Confederate Girlhood.* Unpublished recollections, 1892. [On microfilm in the University of North Carolina collections.]

Stampp, Kenneth. *The Peculiar Institution.* New York: Vintage Books, 1956.

Sweet, Timothy. *Traces of War: Poetry, Photography, and the Crisis of the Union.* Baltimore: The Johns Hopkins University Press, 1990.

Taylor, Louis. *The Story of America's Horses.* Cleveland & New York: World Publishing Company, 1968.

Taylor, Mabel Carver. "First Ladies of Springfield: Mary Whitney Phelps." *Springfield! Magazine.* March 1995.

————. "First Ladies of Springfield: Louisa Cheairs Campbell." *Springfield! Magazine.* Part I, November 1994; Part II, December 1994.

The War of the Rebellion: A Compilation of the Official Records of the Union and Confederate Armies. Series I—Volume III. Washington: Government Printing Office, 1881.

Woodward, C. Vann, ed. *Mary Chestnut's Civil War.* New Haven: Yale University Press, 1981.

Young Adult Civil War Fiction

Beatty, Patricia. *Jayhawker.* New York: Morrow Junior Books, 1991.

Houston, Gloria. *Mountain Valor.* New York: Philomel, 1994.

Keith, Harold. *Rifles for Watie.* New York: Thomas Y. Crowell, 1957.

Lunn, Janet. *The Root Cellar.* New York: Puffin Books, 1981.

Rinaldi, Ann. *In My Father's House.* New York: Scholastic, 1993.